Nov 2019

MOIRAE

MEHREEN AHMED

Moirae

Published by Cosmic Teapot Publishing
Hanmer, ON, Canada
www.cosmicteapot.net

Ordering Information:
Quantity sales. Special discounts are available on quantity purchases by corporations, associations, and others. For details, contact the publisher at the email address above.

Edited by Tony McMahon

Cover art by Maria del mar Garcia Sanchez

Table of Contents

Foreword

Stream of consciousness is a tradition of writing that was made famous in 1922. Also known as interior monologue, this style sets out to tell a story through the internal thought processes of a character. Precursors to this style are seen as early as 1757 in Laurence Sterne's novel, *Tristram Shandy*. Though there are elements of stream of consciousness in *Tristram*, the name of the style wouldn't be coined until 1890. Philosopher, William James, gave it a name, saying of the style, "A 'river' or a 'stream' are the metaphors by which it is most naturally described. *In talking of it hereafter, let's call it the stream of thought, consciousness, or subjective life.*"

In 1922 James Joyce wrote his masterpiece, *Ulysses*, employing the stream of consciousness narrative device. Since then, it has been hailed as one of the most elusive and beautiful writing styles that an author can choose. But because of the difficulties in achieving brilliance in such a demanding narrative voice, only masterful writers choose to take up the call. Virginia Woolf's *Mrs. Dalloway*, William Faulkner's *The Sound and the Fury*, and Samuel Beckett's *Molloy* are a few of the greatest examples.

More recently, and perhaps more closely aligned with *Moirae*'s use of stream of consciousness, Irvine Welsh's *Trainspotting* is an example of how states of dreaming and reality collide together to form a narrative that is not mediated. The character's mind is unfettered by the structure of a regular narrative. As such, even with the double entendre in meaning when Nalia dreams in *Moirae*, we are presented with a truer representation of reality; that is to say, the world is not narrated by a third person. That shift in *Moirae*, of removing the traditional narrator, is the realism that stream of consciousness writing strives for. A story without mediation.

Only the bravest authors tackle the stream of consciousness style. The atmospheric imagery and richly layered language required for stream of consciousness is akin to Picasso's abstract art or John Coltrane's free-form jazz. That is, the unusual phrasing and lack of punctuation create brush strokes and notes of a unique voice. Without pushing at the boundaries of traditional style, the novel would be stuck in a very primitive form. Without literary efforts of authors like Ahmed, the novel would become stagnant.

In the following pages you will read about a planet with two moons, at some point in the future. This world has not changed much: poverty, political corruption, and religious discord divide groups of people. Immigrants that seek a better life are feared and shunned.

Moirae is a dense book packed with literary allusion, existential crises, and personal and public tragedies, told through a unique blend of narrative and stream of consciousness styles, tinged with moments of magic realism.

Ahmed enhances the stream of consciousness segments by eliminating all punctuation, turning sentences into double entendres depending on where you think they should end. "You stupid fool why did you lie so Tell them the truth..." This technique also forces a closer read than if supplied with all the usual markers.

The story follows the plight of a number of characters forced by circumstances to leave their homelands, or commit acts of desperation. It is the story of escape: by boat, or by madness; from one hell to another; from a clear-cut problem, to an empty Kafkaesque nightmare. Simultaneously celebrating the human spirit, while allowing capricious fate to rule, the author elevates the plight of the poor to Greek Tragedy; even, at times, supplying choruses drawn from ancient theater.

Moirae will captivate your imagination and satisfy your need for thought-provoking literary work.

Joe Ferguson

Prologue

In the cold grip of death and high alert, stands the silent land of the Lost Winds. Moral degradation has triggered a mass exodus. Those who were at great risk and in imminent danger have fled the atrocities of the regime by a boat called the Blue Moon to seek protection in a new land. Battling over the high seas through many violent tempests, their sea-unworthy vessel, Blue Moon sailed for days until one evening it was spotted under the roaming beam of the lighthouse on murky waters. The boat has finally reached the shores of Draviland. In the meantime, unfathomable pondering rage in Nalia's head in Lost Winds, as she explores the chaotic, dark fate of her mates. Unpredictable times have created such people, deemed as riders of the howling seas.

"As flies to wanton boys are we to th' gods. They kill us

for their sport- William Shakespeare: King Lear.

Red Tempests

Rain had already begun. Monsoon was unleashed fiercely that morning over Lost Winds, generally known as the village. Impending storm offered no sign of a let up as torrential rain fell from the ashen sky in every direction. Trees swayed, branches creaked and gusty winds lacerated through the tender leaves. Nalia put her knitting down on the chair, under the pumpkin vines to sheaf a broom. She put it together in a bunch with an adhesive around it at the top. Then she swept the throngs of meddling moths of black and grey pebbles off the front yard. The heavy rain pelted steadily down the tip of the serrated fungi, sprawling under the mossy matted fence. Nalia looked at it tentatively, as she finished her morning chore, gathering her clothes neatly over her young, smooth shoulder. She wore a long, cotton untailored piece of cloth wrapped around her like a large sarong. It was a black and white check garb. A call out from a neighbour distracted her slightly, as she turned towards the entrance. Her gaze fell on a girl whose name was Pael. Nalia appeared in the open doorway of her thatched house. She saw that Pael was talking to Shinta.

"My brother has left Lost Winds."

"What? When? Tell me you're joking?"

"No, no I'm not. At 17, he has nothing, no money. Poor soul. Oh! How poor are we?" Pael sobbed.

15

Nalia stood there eavesdropping in silence and looked up at them with a lazy eye. Unexpectedly, she rubbed her snub nose with her palm making it appear even flatter than usual. She found her bearings and looked beyond the entrance, which lent a full view of the rain, like translucent paint on nature's canvas running in rivulets along the gully of the leeches. Nalia picked it up and resumed knitting. She knitted a sweater in honey-comb pattern. With a ball of pink, downy wool under one arm, she walked up to them, closer to the entrance.

"What's up?"

"My father needs to borrow money."

"How much? And why?"

"Why? We need it for my brother," she said. "He needs 100 thousand to pay his Transporters who took him on a boat called Blue Moon into the island of Mundip."

"And why did he need to leave?"

"To get away from police,"

"Police? What police? Tell me. Tell me everything."

"I can tell you only what I know."

"Then tell. What's going on?"

Nalia looked straight at the vertical water lines falling through the curled up wet ferns over a wall of Rhododendrons and Frangipanis. She stood there knitting, listening to her neighbours' ramblings. Her thoughts took her darkly away in a stream of sudden mindlessness.

On the day of her wedding, there were jubilations. Loud music and high-pitched songs were played repeatedly to entertain the wedding guests. Nalia was dressed in cheap silk of sparkly shocking pink. Matching pink slippers looked bright in the afternoon sun, as she stepped out of her father's house into a new heavenly life of the blissful unknown. Little did she know that the cloth wrapped around her was stolen and so were her slippers; flashy studded multicoloured stones, set unevenly on the foot-ware. As darkness fell, an oddity took place which changed her life forever. Under a full marmalade moon, she sat with her wedded husband in a small thatched room. Through the portal of the cane latticed window, she heard the ominous crow lapse into terrible wail, as it flew through the stooping, bunched up bamboo bush. No sooner, men dressed in police clothes kicked open her flimsy wooden door. Befuddled and frightened like a caged experimental mouse, she stood shivering in one corner, as police handcuffed her lover. Then they turned her wedding bed over and ripped through the new, custom made bed that the village mattress-maker had given them as a wedding gift. Gawking, in the candle light, she could not believe her eyes. Police recovered millions of 100s, 50s, and 20s in notes. The money flurried out of the open mattress like the dry leaves of an autumnal maple tree. Accused of robbery, her love was taken and cast away in an ever forbidden hole of a dungeon. Her lazy eye welled up with tears. She wiped them off. Rain poured like a whole heap of tiny white nibbles, straight out of a party bag, in the process of strange metamorphosis.

Her thoughts returned when her neighbours left. She turned around and came back to her room. She felt tired and went to her room for a rest. Unknowingly, as she lay down on her bed, she slipped into slumber. Night fell and she had the strangest dream; she ran, flew and soared, and then fell straight back down, waking with a scream. She crawled up to get herself a glass of water from the aluminium pitcher in the corner of the room. Sounds of the frolicking birds in the moon light of the early morning woke her up. She tried to hear, if the rains had stopped. In that moment every bit of happiness that she ever felt evaporated as rainfall on a parched land.

It was in shame that she returned to her father's house, after her husband had been arrested. Each day she hoped for a miracle to happen and went without a meal for days. Hair uncombed, without a shower, she even surpassed banshees in looking her worst. She too had a brother once. Not being able to endure her affliction of separation from her husband any longer, he had hatched a plan in a sudden frenzy to help her.

Brother had decided to borrow heavily from a wealthy farmer to bribe the police for her husband's acquittal. He nearly succeeded. The wealthy man agreed to lend him 50 thousand in cash, but not unconditionally. It was a debt, of a most horrible kind. The brother could not pay it back. The farmer forced him to work on his rice fields without payment. It wasn't an acceptable proposition. Brother decided to flee. On natural impulse, he desired freedom from this slave labour. Nalia heard a cough coming from the next room; her father lay snoring like a fat old cat. She called him, but didn't hear a response. She looked out at the morning afterglow streaming in through the matted window. She rose from her bed creeping quietly on the floor toward her belongings. Opening the lid of a black, battered suitcase, she drew out a beat-up tin of biscuits with a tightly pressed lid. With some effort she wrung it open. In it, there was some money, 500 only in cash, which she had found accidentally on that fate less wedding night after the police had left. It slipped somehow sitting in a shadowy corner to be picked up. Happy in the belief that one day she would be able to buy comfort, she put it in the suitcase tucked under the few clothes that she had, before she left this life behind her. Without anyone to care for, she had not much clothes and no jewellery at all. In all the world she only possessed 500 gold coins. Whatever relationship she had with the man, this husband of hers, was over. Her marriage was now over. The 50, 000 borrowed to free him from police had also gone unaccounted for and was now needed to pay off the farmer, which the brother had owed or else he would be confined to unpaid slavery for life. Distraught by her sibling borrowing heavily and then trying to buy her life back, she was just as helpless as her parents to save him out of this troubled situation. They could never pay off this debt. Money and poverty was the root of all her worries. Trepidation filled her up. The next morning, Nalia thought of her ugly life. She walked down the Murma river. The newspapers had said it all. That her husband was caught off the coast of the Panuma Island, selling riders to Transporters, people who agreed to organise illegal passage for a payment into the land of Dravi. Her brother was gone that way too. She sat down on the bank of the Murma River and weeded nettles from an over grown grassy patch. Strange, she could not find any flowers in the lowland of the river bank. Silvery waves dulled under the grey cloud. It was going to rain again. She looked up. Her brother was gone. Yes, but his boat had capsized near the shores of the Siren peninsula. And that was that. It was one of the lucky stories. Boats always sank in the deep seas near the Underworld. Miraculously, they were rescued by Dolphins; the hapless people of the boat lived. Incredible indeed. The night was cold and so was the water. It was murky too when their boat sank as it proceeded through the Underworld Mountain range. Their legs constantly walked the waters under the sea; fear and panic seized them, as they heard their own shallow breathing. They looked around but encountered fury on every uncompromising lap of the waves. Children never made it back and adults were ready to embrace death just when a few survivors floated up on the bosom of the sea. They were suddenly encircled by Dolphins in the shark infested ocean while predators roamed at large on the outer circle. Dolphins sheltered them as their own. Stories went a bit further, to say that these Dolphins, their saviours, even guided them to safety. They waded with them to the nearest island spotted within the radius of the beam from the light house where the ocean slapped those very shores in gentle wavering movement. Towards the light house, the Dolphins then swam away afterwards. And that was the tale of survival that seeped slowly into the village. Would fortune be with her neighbour's brother too? He had also left. What if perchance, his boat also sank, and he was left with the sharks alone? A shiver went straight up her spine. Since that day, Nalia feared the worst. She feared for Pael's brother and for all those people who were leaving the village for one reason or the other. She was not on any boat, but was still in the village, safely enveloped within the shrubbery of banana plants and jack fruit trees. Circumstances will pull her toward a unique destiny, percolating beyond control perhaps. Her job was to continue to dream for that day, when she would become self-sufficient. God knows, she was not wealthy, but she was at least free.

Monsoon rain eased off a bit. The last of the rain water, dripped lazily down the tea leaves from the plantation along the river. Distant drizzles were a mass of tiny fluids poised spectacularly on air. Nalia got up and walked home warily; not sure if she would sleep well that night. Extending an arm down, she wrung little yellow flowers off the edge of the dirt path. These looked lovely, 'blushed many a times to die unseen', as many a times as the people in the village. Hapless victims ran away for reasons they were not responsible for. Human fate was strange. Stranger still was human dilemma.

Seventeen-year-old boy had escaped. His father's arch enemy, Miah had framed him for an alleged murder. It had not stopped there. What was his name? Pontu, Pael's brother. He left home in search of a new life, on a new soil on a journey through Mundip.

Poor Pontu. He was not wealthy, neither was his father. Look, what happened? Born in poverty, he was surrounded by vile people from childhood, who ensnared him in a murder case. A trap. Goodness me. Fleeing from one place to another was what he did all his life. The regime tried to recruit him to do the dirty jobs for them. When he did not want to do it, they beat him up;

when he joined them, they played him; tied him to this murder case; an unspeakable crime committed by another. What other option was left? The police had even arrested Pontu once, but he was able to escape from jail. He would be arrested again, he knew, in Mundip. Courage and optimism led him on, so he would live to the fullness of life. If only the wheel of fortune turned for the better. One lucky break was all that this lad needed. Being illegal, there were great uncertainties, as vast as the ocean itself. Anxiety gripped him like wet hair strand coiled around a finger hard to shake the moisture off. To be happy and to be safe were his basic rights, but he struggled to have even that. A child was always born in innocence until forces of circumstances snatched it away. It happened all too soon for him, happened almost in his infancy, at 17, only 17.

Reminiscence of her own life spoke again to her of how her marriage had ended before it was even consummated. 16 and she had barely put her foot forth into the world. Henna still fresh on her palms seemed to scream out for justice in brick red. Her entire being cried out of ingrown aches of unfulfilled love. She must get away. Get her life back together before it ended. Life would end sooner than people thought. Up in the sky, clouds continued to manifest in dramatic moody hues. Tinges of crimson glowed momentarily, before masses of ink and grey crowded in. Constable's sky would not have looked more poetic on its canvas with such a spillage of riotous colours. Vapours crossed broodingly about in emptiness, right before a melt-down. Quick lightening crept through unpredictably in toothed lines, followed by bellows from heavens above. Nalia began to run like a petrified black gazelle.

Funds needed to be raised. She walked past Pontu's house and saw them eating. 100,000 was a far cry, when even one remained to be seen. Pontu would languish in some hellish hole for being illegal. But the Transporters must be paid in full or else this journey could be a futile one and not end up in Dravi. Dodging bullets, pastings from police and captures lay further ahead for Pontu in Mundip. Oh. How awful. He had only just turned 17. Nalia glimpsed at them briefly. Through the open portal, she saw them packing huge balls of fermented soaked rice in water. Radish and rice on their palms was galvanised straight out of an earthen bowl into their gaping hungry mouths. Hunger gave them insatiable appetite, anyway; fuelled by nervousness today, slowing down of the jumpy finger to mouth motion was impossible. Their son rafted on some remote corner of the Red Seas, and they were in the iron grips of bleak powerlessness.

Nalia slowed down her pace. Something needed to be done about her life too. It was not her desire to end up in the slave market or some big pleasure houses. Options were limited. She was not a defeatist. At 16 she did not want to be one. Perhaps, she could fall in love again. Her friend Tahu, worked in a garment factory in the city. She remarried soon after her first husband perished under the rubbles, when another garment factory collapsed.

Nalia picked up a tune from a movie translated as *The Claybird*. Forlorn and sleepless, she lay in her bed lamenting next to her parent's room. These walls held no secrets back, as she heard them talk.

"100,000 is a lot of money."

"They must sell the milk cow and raise the money," A women's voice sounded desperate.

"We could have given them a loan," her father said,

"But we're hard-up ourselves."

Nalia got up from her bed and went to sit on the dirt floor in the front yard. The moon didn't shine tonight. Sallow light from the hurricane lamp imparted almost a surreal, magical luminescence in the darkness. She heard her mother's muffled voice.

"I wish Nalia would get married again. That would be one less mouth to feed."

"Speak softly, I don't want her to hear this," warned Nalia's father.

And then there was silence. Nalia knew what was expected of her. But she loved him, the one that she had married and he loved her so. But he was gone now. Tahu was different, the banal kind; the kind that did not procrastinate. She did what she had to do. Love was never an issue for her. But Nalia? Would she be able to love again? Her best friend Tahu lived in the city. She left village a while ago, about two years now. She could find her a job in the garment factory in the city. She made up her mind to find work in just such a place, like Tahu and many of those young girls leaving the village. The native's full innocence beguiled her. She was going to leave a pristine life behind to look for Tahu in the city and embark on a life of the unknown, not having the slightest clue of what awaited her. In one short move, she latched on to this new exciting idea of the city full of adventure. Little did she know what she was getting into? The maddening rat race of the city knocked her over. She confronted here the most heinous of crimes. Reality today would have been different than what it turned out to be. Fate had pushed her towards something she was helpless in resisting. Great expectations turned into unbearable misery, so much so that her plights led to muddled thoughts of an absurdist sporadic mind.

At first she couldn't find her friend Tahu in the city, not until much later anyway. At her wit's end, Nalia was engaged in deep monologue one summer's day knitting her long sweater in the

26

city of Grosnii, as her mind continued to travel randomly nonlinear across space and time; she contemplated on wretched occurrences happening not only in her life, but also in those of her friends. Echoes of the past raced through her head which offered reconnaissance of the time, quite out of joint.

Ash Woodlands

Dizzy Dizzying pace Grosnii was a place where dreams came true In the city I walked the footpaths by the parliament building Properties appreciate here in the city Look for work Tahu was settled in her job I brushed her hair in Tahus little shack In the village I got up to eat breakfast The boat was waiting I got on The boat began to sail City was crowded Oh my My so many people Getting on Almost squeezed in the boat People once too many Tahu where was she in this humdrum No address Mother you werent here with me in the city Lost I am completely Lost I am drowning The boatman was but a boy The storm boat was sinking I was sinking mother and my father Tahu I was sinking The city was crowded but I searched to find Tahu No impossible village was much safer Oh no no let me go you bastards let me go Do you think I was your whore I came from village looking for work Tahu worked in garment factory The job was good I could send money to the village Tahu let me stay here I needed money more and more Not enough I was hungry in the village No money Evening passed into night In the street of the city I walked home to find Tahu Horrible Blood Pain On the street five men on top of me one after another I was in gang rape A victim How shameful Shame In the village the Murma flowed unheeded I sat in the front yard in the morning Mother made breakfast I had some bread I couldnt stop crying Property prices were good in the City I had nothing to lose now Nothing Paels brother Pontu in Mundip His sister said so 100 thousand cash payment was needed Pontu was in jail Mundipian Police caught him Pontu was kept in a house full of eight Hingyan riders Pontu escaped In the deep jungles of Mundip he climbed up trees to hide Police in the darkness of night found Pontu Terrible beatings Bribery Pontu was still in prison Poor boy Fled from the country Alleged murder case Where would Pontu go Who could save him Money where was money coming from No food Hungry Pontu was asleep on the cold floor Hard knock on the door woke him The police were here Mundip Hurt Oh how it hurt They were beating Pontu for more and more information He had given them all he had There was no more to give Lie said the agent Lie or else they would send you back to the village I sat brushing my hair on the front yard of my home in the Lost Winds The boat was caught up in the storm the boat boy saved me I was found unconscious on the bank of the river Murma Tahu in city was getting ready to go to work She cooked fish Packed it up in lunch box Now on her way to work Her new husband looked at her and said dont be late Where is yesterdays money gone Under the bed Why Dont go squandering it drinking What is it to you Ill beat the hell out of you Tahus husband took a belt and put two lashes on her back OOOH Here take it take the money Tahu was pregnant The child was still safe in her womb Villagers were here I have been shamed in the city I have been in gang rape Tahu or her husband could not save me Why it wasnt my fault What was my fault mother and father Could you have saved me Save me from those bastards They came to kill me They came to take me away to sell me into prostitution Back on the boat I was on my way to the city Again Tahu would take care of me I would work as domestics cook and clean for people in the city Me I told meself Forget about property forget about garment factory forget about everything Pontu was languishing in Mundipian prison Transporters sold freedom to people like Pontu Told him he must lie to them he must tell them that economic crisis made him a rider Pontu sought freedom in Mundip Police were looking for him in the jungle they wanted bribe Hid behind the tree It was night time He was very quiet Squatted like an animal like a cat on all fours The police had gone He made a plank for himself in the jungle to sleep on with whatever branches twigs he found in the dark woods under dense tree Lucky that snakes did not get him I made bed for meself in the slip lane off one of the city streets The distant mountains looked like a series of corrugated shadow against the backdrop of a blood smeared evening Bloody evening sky A lonely boat travelled on the ocean of huge waves Headed in search of new land A child was born incognito People threw up everywhere No land was visible No No

Conflict of free will and pre-destination; what choices could this child exercise that he was born on a boat full of riders destined to go God knows where ...?

The child It was on this boat not in pain Yet he had needs Tahu was in pain In city she was at a hospital where her baby was born Unloved child born in poverty In the slums A product of domestic quarrel A kind of rape This child who would never see wealth Tahu cried along with the baby The love child No not at all Marriage did not always make love children I waited for my lover by the Murma river One day a boat would come and my lover would get off Mother would I be happy again In city domestics were paid quite well I should get a good job Mother I had a beautiful house in Shingdi a vegetable garden Vines of bitter gourd lettuce English spinach and tousled coconut trees Coconuts fell on my darling husbands head One day we made love under the tree Now I was pregnant just like my orchard full of fruits with the love child Oh I ran as hard as I could from the shadow These were shadows of time shadows of the past I woke up A dream The sun was going down over the horizon of the Murma river in the village from where my brother left Pontu left Dolphins saved my brother on those rough seas Tumultuous waves on the sea I was heartbroken Brother ran away from that vampire of a farmer and Pontu for his alleged murder Mother would they be happy again In city you struggled to deliver the baby Tahu in the berthing suite of the hospital Tahu your baby

31

boy born into marriage but out of love In Shingdi My baby boy

would have been born he would have had a loving home My

husband my love we loved each other so much He kissed me on

the cheek first and then on the lips He whispered into my ears

your red ruby lips drives me crazy I laughed I was happy with my

family in Shingdi Mother I wept as I made my bed on the

streets in the city Every night men came and they did bad things

to me One day Mother I too will fall pregnant Oh what would I

do then with the child A child who would hang down my waist

like a clinger Malnourished Mother I so need a home to stay Beg

An unsightly beggar I wish I could go to Mundip with Pontu

Brother came out of the house of God one day on Wellington

road in the city of Troy The priests were with him He found

peace in Dravi philosophy Their Religion of Jesuit faith in one

God His friends have stopped talking to him One friend looked

at him full of hatred was his best friend too One who travelled

on the same boat over the high seas Walking on Wanji streets in

Troy Brother brought some flowers to carry to the house of God

service At the alter there were candles and flowers where the

priest also stood giving his sermons Brother took lessons

wanted to live a happy life The wealthy farmer nearly got him

He had people visiting him in the village demanding money or

else they would kill him Money 50,000 was a lot of money

father Told him not to call on his mobile again He became a

Dravi Loved prophet Jesuit Not prophet Mohammadan He loved

his life more A freedom seeker in Troy Brother thought must convert What if he still did not qualify to become a freedom seeker His friends looked at him weirdly Five people stayed in one room Two in each bed placed side by side One on the floor on a mattress He didnt have to convert He didnt want to be a Mohammadan any more He loved the Jesuits now as much as he loved his life He loved He went to the house of God from now on Finished worshipping and boys came out of the Mahammadan house of God in droves wearing white long dresses looking like moving refrigerators and heads covered in round cotton caps hugging the shape of their heads That was the noon worship that the village men had gone that afternoon Those were more peaceful times when they felt peace at heart Peace in the universe and towards neighbours Men turned up in Honda wearing sun glasses that one child in the village called *Library Sunnys* Teenagers were asked to work for the regime Recruitment was taking place Brother cleaned his teeth Friends have eaten dinner but have not asked him to join them for dinner In their home on Wanji street in Troy Brother became stronger He resisted he avoided looking at them Dravi priests brought peace to his mind and to his life No more recruitment My wedded husband was found in jail Brother went up to him to ask him Why he would soon be out He would bribe his way out of jail Pontu would bribe the police He has had enough of it Mundip police took the bribe but was still unrelenting Pontu got beaten up one more time for being an illegal in Mundip Pontu worked as an Illegal Mundipian Transporter paid in full Pontu vomited on the high seas over the boat rail The new born baby looked at him Pontu smiled Tahu also smiled at her new born in her slum dwelling Husband entered drunk at night and beat her up The baby was malnourished so was she There was no milk in her bosom for the baby She lost her job at the garment factory Along the Murma river the wooden boat cruised Tahu gave the baby a water burial She wept until her tears dried up Yet there were more More tears flowed There were no safe houses for people like us Poor Born in Poverty Raped The rich mans daughter in the city said she hated her expensive wedding sari All this jewellery but loved only her shoes Strangely She was married to a multi millionaire who owned five Mercedes Benz She was covered from top to toe in Diamonds Glittering diamonds were forever and so was this bride supposed to be Thats what the groom thought anyway I heard him say jokingly to his friends Thats why he covered her with so many sparkling diamonds Rich girl married to a rich man There was no end to food and jewellery The house was full of them and expensive perfume wafted through the air I started work mother I worked in this house in my cheap sari Pretty I was Pretty too The rich girl just left with her new husband in expensive car Wedding was now over In Shingdi I sat down with my knitting I loved knitting honey comb pattern in pink yarn for my baby yet to be

born My baby mother Was this dream ever going to be real
mother I woke up in Shingdi I worked as a domestics in this
wealthy house in city doing dishes scrubbing floors cooking
running errands Tired Slept In Shingdi there were lovely flowers
What lovely flowers They were Gardanias Sunflowers and Roses
I bought some for Tahu back in the village Tahu sat crying in her
house in village I brushed her hair well I brushed her mad hair
Tahu was losing it Sanity she just lost her baby A baby lay
smiling at Pontu in her mothers lap on the boat of the heaving
waves Tired but the happy mother nursed it My husband
mother walked the streets of Mundip I was awakened from
sleep One night he called me on the mobile let go let go of
everything Put it all in the past and move on It was never meant
to be It was such a farce my marriage with this man He too fled
from the police in Mundip he just saw one police and
disconnected the phone abruptly Never meant to be mother
Where could I go Villagers would not let you be in peace
because of me They had a meeting saying I am bad bad to the
bone I am not Not my fault I never asked for any of this to
happen mother Im but 16 Brother flossed his teeth in the
bathroom he must move out of Wanji street he had enemies
now his friends had become his enemies his family too for
converting he did this for survival but he loved Jesuits Three
years on Those pretty diamonds couldnt keep the rich girl the
bride tied up to her rich husband in the big house in the city In

Londau she sat having coffee twirling her pony tails flirting with her new lover Husband sat in the quiet city room in oblivion of the Sordid affair Money corrupted she said she wanted to visit a friend Indeed he kissed her red lips They lay between those sweaty sheets in his bed Bodies entwined For hours his carriage ran though the congestion clogged up traffic in city He was going to send more money to his bride the girl he had married and covered with diamonds

boyfriend in Londau will take it all, will take all, would have cried the chorus of Sophocles in Oedipus Rex. Blasphemy, adultery. She spoke of loyalty with a forked tongue.

I just finished my chores in her mothers house How the world jilted me The clock struck two in morning they should wake up soon Tea will then be served at the bed with sweet biscuits I slept By the river Murma a boat came sailing down A boy rowed it wearing a patched white

shirt as he sang in foreign tongue.

"I'm so tired of life that I can't row this boat any longer; pick up the oars o the captain of my soul..."

Shrill telephone sounds woke her up In Londau a terrible accident had claimed the lives of two people Car crashed They were in hospital Nurses in their starch white gowns and bluecaps attended to the patients in the emergency No no no the flat line on the computer screen said it all And that was that The nurses were sad the world was shocked as shocked as the parents where I worked as domestics The husband sat in his Mercedes in the traffic What a terrible tragedy But who was the Man with the rich girl Questions remained unanswered One two three four I count with my fingers Days gone by Life returned to normalcy Mother I dont want to die at 16 Could I live here in the village with you and father A walk by the river Murma I wanted to live by the Murma It was the burial place for Tahus little baby What else would it witness Villagers would kill me eventually They think I shamed them Mother city is not a place for single young girl Tahus husband was in jail for robbery She stopped eating and drinking I wanted to live with you Mother Monsoon in the village is greener No trees in the city Rain looks strange and gloomy Tahu was pretty and Pael too Men left in droves Mother what would happen to the rich girls jewellery she got when she wedded Now maybe a newcomer would have them Some some lucky girl would make this unfortunate man happy Wedding bells are ringing already mother I hear them as I see diamonds glitter everywhere once again In the city Shadows cover the streets and knives smeared with blood shine in the darkness of these alleys Mad It is a mad world Wedding lights are the colours of the rainbow again Mother I wouldnt want my life to end at 16 no matter what No matter how many times I have been raped These are mother the unforetold miseries of our times.

Black Streams

Very well We could have had a good life in Shingdi living off the land We had even planned a home Children would have grown up by now I wail sitting by the Murma river but your baby is gone Tahu You could have woken me up when cocks crowed at dawn We could have had tea and molasses together under the shack of a house You wanted to return to the wifebashingthief of a husband of yours It was but a hornets nest a far cry from Shingdi A paradise a dream which would never have materialised By far it could have been the most beautiful life Why could we not have tea at dawn with molasses Tahu you should have had that bastard beaten to death your husband Oh your husband lay under those blistering rubbles there There should be money to day Snatched someone elses land Wife bashing husband of yours murderer of your child You ate the best dinner tonight Tahu should we take a walk along the Murma You saw him You saw your child Its face resurfaced on the water He called you Oh how hungry he must be by now You should go to your baby He loved the river Murma Dont hold me back now How you cried out Tahu Doctors pills Why could we not go back to city together By now we could have had a new life just you and me Me I am still pretty I could get married again have children in Shingdi Isnt that the place where our hearts were set Our homes That was the place where we should have been We could have been here if it had not been for that man who robbed you Your child Tahu Money So much Money you gave that bastard Everything you ever earned and this was how he treated you Should we have some tea on the bank of the Murma Your tiny baby was hungry Tahu you heard cries of hunger pain That bastard wanted you to give him all Tipped em out like beans out of bean pods How much was enough Enough was enough no more no less Shingdi was the place to be Tahu where ripe juicy mangoes grew in abundance Our life was like one short summers day Life Sweet Why would I die I didnt want to die I found work Told you so Work Divorce that bastard Oh here it comes again the baby cried straight out of the river Murma You saw it Tahu not just once but many times Pretty ladies in Grosnii were having tea and coffee in Coffee Place Expensive cars in the city Shingdi by far was the best Tahu Riders were perhaps waking up in Botany Bay Clocks struck eight o clock in the morning Oh my God my brother had just missed his appointment with his lawyer He must learn Kroll language fast Go to house of God Be a good boy Coping in the city was hard for me Soon I realized that this was not my place Pillage in the next suburb claimed lives of many Botany Bay was where riders lived off the coast of the Panuma Island Terrible how killing mugging bloody spillage were now all a part of our normal life Tahu What a joke peace had become Joke People have forgotten about peace They craved for peace No Then why were people leaving in droves if they did not crave peace Tahu Could you give me one good reason why Pontu and my brother could not have stayed here in the village Shingdi would have been the right place Not Botany Bay Madura Island what did it matter Well now Pontu woke up in his bed in Madura Island Someone was shot here tonight at the boot camp The media everybody anybody even the high counsellor himself could not help him Only 23 years old The boy died He died Guards killed him Unarmed No place to hide here Bad thing A bullet pierced through him blood thick red Young Pillage Plunder in the boot camp Madura Island boot camp was where Pontu was hiding under the bed now Afraid The rough seas Mundip Alleged murder of Miahs nephew to be precise now he hid under the bed in Madura Island boot camp Well now he was in the grips of fear with 40 other riders were detained hiding under the bed Brother in Botany Bay walked the street on his way to house of God Tahu did you have plans What plans did you have if any at all How many times a day did you pray Five times or not even once Tahu but I am done Done I have nothing to lose Clothes were everywhere all over the floor He had better choose something to wear Black Suits were on the bed on the floor Tahu I told you I put them back in the wardrobe The master of the house could not decide what he wanted to wear tonight His daughter perished in a car crash in Londau He and his wife must put flowers on her grave The streets of Londau seemed all the

same to them as they walked with flowers in their hands By
Jove they must be lost among all those in black coats Cold
Londau was cold Tahu That was what they told me then
"Poor Tom's a-cold," cried one character in Shakespeare's King
Lear, across Trafalgar Square past the double-decker red bus.
a bouquet of flowers Red Roses wilted at the altar of the
daughters grave Leaves flew dry in the cold draft Soup was for
dinner tonight in Madura Island boot camp Pontu sat down to
dinner But he craved fish and green hot chillies and coriander
Maa That was Pontus mother Tahu Pontu told his maa I dont
eat that stuff no more I wished No maa No dont you cry again
Something good will happen soon Okay I will try and make a life
for meself here I will go to Botany Bay I must learn Kroll Learn it
Go to Kroll classes Pontu said to the guards in Madura Island
Run run away Run as far as you can run up and down the curve
of the world Run his maa said but Tahu Pontu was exhausted by
now He was back to the finish line where he had started No way
out He could run no more There was no way out of this God
forsaken place The Madura Island boot camp

Pontu continued to be trained here in the Madura Island boot
camp waiting for order, waiting for Godo as it were. This order
would release him. Uncertainty loomed large. He lied following
the Transporter's advice. They told him, he must suppress the
murder allegation or else he would be in danger of being
deported. He said he came because of crop failure every year in

the Lost Winds. There was no food. The moment he said this, his case was knocked back. He should have spoken the truth. That would have been in his best interest. That was what causing the delay. Pontu was confused. Surely, there was more to life than this. An afterlife was perhaps better than this tedium. There was a sense of freedom in that. Was God, watching over them? No, there was none; nothing; living creatures had been dumped into a hot cauldron, called the earth which was just like the boot camp itself and that was it. It ended here with no exits. In this infinite cycle of life, after death, one became dust or ash in an urn and that was the final destination. That ultimate infinity, was found in this metamorphosis. No sweet angels sang in heavens above for the hapless souls. What lies? The notions of heaven and hell, purgatory, sin and redemption were the biggest lies that there ever were.

I did not yet finish knitting my pink sweater in honeycomb pattern My husband would have loved it He would have worn it It would have been finished by now No it was still going Continued Tahu I wouldn't know when this knitting would stop Down by the river Murma the raindrops descended in frightening density The river swelled too Far too much water in its belly The small boat struggled to keep up in the storm Tahu I went to the knitting store to buy loads of pink yarn Who made a mistake Did you just push me Tahu I laughed that day heavy with storm A man had looked at me and had given me a peck on the cheek Dont The Mohammadans the guardians of the Mahammadan faith would have sent a stern message Under the guava tree on the open bank of the Murma river we two would have dated Dream of Shingdi was a dream of a lifetime He had said No I dont like you I love you Your red bangles your pretty garb your little painted feet How I want to marry you You had said What at 15 I could have eloped I married too soon 16 Oh for Gods sake dont take this dream away Let me dream At the grave yard in Londau the rich girls mother wept for the loss The father wept too for the loss But little did they know that their girl was not faithful to her husband The one that had given her jewellery and expensive clothes I wept for your loss too This husband took all your stuff and beat you You woke up and walked Clothes in disarray It fell off your shoulders asked me for tea No amount of tea made you feel better this morning You looked around your shack in the slum Husband was away for now The cup of tea needed more sugar How was I going to cope with this grief Groggy I felt really groggy my eyes squinted and swollen as I looked around your shack A bed was made on the plank Pills on the tilted table with a broken leg The table was covered with an old dated yellow tinged newspaper Tea needed more sugar you put two pills in your mouth and swallowed them with the Tea Water gushed out from a broken pipe flooding the alley of the slum from an unknown source Sleep walked down the alley I needed to arrange my clothes What a beautiful winter morning You were 18 on your way to work packed a lunch of fish fries on rice On the other side of the Garment factory not far Friends were here Waited for you You walked up the road together and entered the building Five long hours in the factory sewing clothes for the big brand companies No more You languished Tahu Could you feed the baby Baby had gone to a much better place now You cried Oh Boundless Tears Not dried up yet It never would

"O that this too too sullied flesh..."

Do you want to eat something I shall leave the city soon go away from this awful place Property prices were good in the city Well not anymore Not at all What was keeping you Tahu I was awakened this morning by a horrible scream I saw it It was not a dream No Tahu It was not Turn on the lights Please Let there be some light Lights More lights Oh this was such a dark place a dungeon By now Pontu went to bed Tahu thinking when he might be released from the boot camp in Madura Island The day went quite well Some progress was made Talks with officers here in their stark offices Across the table questions were shot that Pontu had no answers for How did he get here Why had he come What route did he take Pontu you needed to lie Pontu was sweating under that shirt He lied Telling a lie or misleading an officer was an offence Pontu could not hear them properly He lied He escaped because he was poor who rode the Red Sea

44

for repeated droughts and pestilence Not quite though he wanted to live a life that he couldnt in the village You stupid fool why did you lie so Tell them the truth Tell them what really happened that your life fell apart No the Transporters in Mundip said this place was only for Hingyans not for us Lie Pontu Lie Dont lie lying will not get you anywhere But Pontu didnt want to be in Madura This was a creepy place Pontu cried Dont worry maa I should be able to send you money soon No need to pay off the Transporter He nearly got caught in Mundip but he lived in the forest for seven long days and night One day he came out and saw a man in police clothes He bribed him heavily Next he was sitting in this room with five other riders from God knows where Tahu he must be on that boat That boat *Blue Moon* meant freedom He thought he was free Tahu He felt he soared like a falcon Oh but it was not where he was supposed to be He was not quite there yet But the Transporters lied They took the money and they said they were on their way to freedom to Draviland But no It was hard much harder than he thought Tahu 16 months still in Boot camp Still at Madura Pontu sat in his room in the village He should have been employed by now Something He was engaged to something allright Only the gym and Kroll classes and military training It was such a beautiful bright summer morning Oriental Magpie Robins flew high up in the sky with not a shred of cloud anywhere Larks and Mynas together huddled on that Banana leaves there Hugging a toy house with arms around it A boy came running from behind asking Pontu to flee Yes he must run away through the narrow passage by the Mohammadan house of God Miah must back off Someone else killed his nephew not Pontu That fateful night the nephew slept peacefully in his room A terrified shriek sliced through the night All night birds were awakened In shock By now neighbours were already in Miahs house

No, oh No, this has not been mete out with poetic justice, the chorus of Aeschylus would have cried out in horror.

What a terrible sin A sin was about to be occurred Murdered Butchered was Miahs nephew Very well then lets go after Pontu the child of innocence who slept away in another house One who knew nothing

Disease, death and suffering broke out in the village, flowing like the black river of   pestilence. Horror! What utter horror! Shocking!

Police were pitiless Tahu Pontus little house was full of people in uniform Pontu was gone Sheer pandemonium Pontus mother cried out Pael cried too So did the father Pael must still be quite unsettled although Pontu has reached safely to Madura Island Money had been paid Not so fast Pontu was apprehended by the police in the city for the murder Threats and violence in the boot camp was where

"Light thickens."

46

fights broke out Pontu could not escape from this mandatory training He was able to bribe his way through so far Now he was wedged here for 16 months He could very well have a good life here eating drinking and sleeping Hingyans off the south seas themselves had been threatened all their lives in their Southern Kingdoms Perhaps on their way to the neighbouring country as well Those who could not access education or medical facilities in their own country of birth The three year old boy who was left behind when his parents fled to safety In fear and panic the little boy cried his lungs out Another man in that chaotic wave of human exodus picked him up Tahu he was not the brother that I thought he was although he was brought up as one Tahu he was well loved by father who found the earthling by the sea when he went fishing one day By Jove he was famished by then Well his chest was heaving from fear Yet once again father picked him up and brought him to our house where he grew up Mother and father gave him sustenance Jesuit priests sat with this adult orphan at Botany Bay house of God reading the great Jesuit Book of faith and educating him Nuns and priestesses have possibly given him shelter now that all his Mohammadan friends have deserted him for becoming a Jesuit Another life carved out for this boy in another world And in this other world woe was the nickname of todays people fleeing all kinds of persecution Luckily though when father found him alone Tahu weeping by the sea he was barely three years of age Under the street lamp at Botany Bay clandestine activities were registered by guards Working at a much lower rate here Exploitation No permits to work My brother told father and mother Tahu People were picked up from the boat *Blue Moon* by guards Ended up in another world where they had not intended to be

Dob In. Dob them in, the chorus of Sophocles of Oedipus Rex might have said. I say, don't dob them in. The crown is in the gutter, Let them pick it up. If they don't someone else would. That is the only way the less fortunate survive. What would you have done?

Romeo Romeo oh where were you now Wailing would not bring my Romeo back My beloved husband Caught in an act of negligent secret dealing by the river Murma My Romeo was arrested by the regime Dont lie If you were caught lying would lead to terrible punishment was the repeated message from the authorities Tahu but Pontu said No no I no lie no lying never no I in no trouble before No Kroll Sorry Poor soul was thrown back in the boot camp for lying Permits cancelled for lying Terrible punishments loomed

Stop. Did the British not lie in India? Did they not say that they had come with a trade offer, when they had actually come to colonise? Lies in the newspeak of 1984 were the greatest lies of all. Free. Did this word 'free' have ambiguous meanings? Did it mean freedom? No, it only meant if the dog was free of lice. Political freedom, a dirty word in Crimethink, meant something

48

else. Why was this word even there then in newspeak
dictionary? If it did not mean what 'freedom' was supposed to
have meant. What deception! What treachery!

Who didnt lie Tahu You braided my hair in the slum It laid
heavily on my backbone with a tail at the end You took out a
white and a blue pill out of the jar and popped them into your
mouth Then I poured meself a glass of water from the black
shiny pitcher placed in the corner of the fungus smeared floor
Pontu was happy At least he was alive within these walls of the
boot camp for Pontu would have been in jail and hanged by
now in his homeland What was the use of fretting He felt less
Anxious and could see lights at the end of the tunnel Something
new happened Pontu would be given a chance to reapply to the
authorities to allow him to stay in Draviland Tahu when he
clearly thought he would not He was denied Mission
unsuccessful Terrified He hid He hid under that bed Frightful
night Men being killed by guards in the Madura Island he did
not think even for once that he would live but he lived guards
got him out The waves on the ocean flowed in a direction he
had not understood which pathway to take My thoughts flowed
unhindered unimpeded The mind could go wherever Do
whatever In a moment I was in the Lost Winds now eating fish
Next I was on the street of the city puking into a storm water
drain The newborn looked at Pontu and smiled again Curlews

unfettered cries brought him back to the boot camp His life was uncertain and so was his pathway If this was not how else could he have escaped Lucky that Pontu didnt die like the other rider Shot as he tried to save himself What an irony Riders came here to escape persecution but died in the hands of their saviour Oh what woeful fate His life Tahu There were always celebrations in Shingdi the land of plenty Generosity poured out of peoples hearts here Warmth and affection No affliction A big feast a great harvest Beggars sat in a row in front of a big house that belonged to another wealthy farmer Rich in every aspect this farmer fed the poor of Shingdi out of the generosity A big cow had been slaughtered last night Cooked in a huge big Cauldron with massive serves of rice caked on each tin plate and a glass of water on the side of the sitting mats on the floor Oh how good it tasted Gravy beef piping red hot on hot hot rice cakes. The poor of Shingdi celebrated life Prayed for the rich so they would go to heaven after death Eating was happiness The poor was believed to be much closer to God than the rich While the high counsellor deliberated over a decision Brother read the Jesuit Book of faith A ticket to freedom That was what he thought at least By the Mohammadan house of God you saw me walk A dirt path Suddenly a pair of strong hands held me tightly Oh A love smile appeared on those lips of mine These were the bygone days Spots of time spent with my Romeo Look what I bought he had said What did you buy I looked up with a glint in my eyes A pair of red bangles Was this what you were doing as I waited for you in our spot

The mind was a powerful apparatus, after all.

I wished to see him and there he was with a gift in his hand I didnt think I was going to see you today No Well here I was had been to the fair Oh lucky you You could have taken me along I could have but I wanted it to be a surprise What innocent days were those Tahu carefree and pure Pure it hurt so much oh those awful moments on the streets Under the lamp post in the city Those men took what I valued most I lost it to the rapists and everyone who had me at night on the streets I cried Tahu Needed to see mother too Soon This big house was stifling It smelled of death Sweet smell of death Diamond girl buried in Londau Lonesome in this big house Would the religious leaders in the village ever forgive me Would I not ever be forgiven My Romeo could have taken me away from this woe but he told me it was not meant to be over the phone And that this was a regrettable mistake Awful Awful He would have to own up to me one day He cut my life too short Rain was starting beautifully over the horizon A storm was coming in soon Tahu The dog cried in despair A stray dog He had no shelter Do you have shelter Where would I have gone in this rain if I had not been hired in this house Tahu This house It was a lucky house I think it was a safe house The lightening had just crossed the sky Reflection on the mirror told me I stood in front of it Showed a beautiful young girl of 16 already burdened with pressures of life Huge black rings around the eyes Eye bags Why were people afraid of death It came naturally to everyone Why did people feel sad when others died They would join them soon anyway Oh Look at that sporadic lightening speared through the starless sky of pitch darkness I am not afraid Not quite All those little boys came out of the Mohammadan house of God after the noon worship They went running around the house of God playing hide and seek They hid from one and another

In this great cycle of life and death, one needed to hide. Hide from authorities. They would never make anyone rich but entrap, ensnare, and enslave one in the codes of religion. Hide, hide away. Spiritualism was different. It meant freedom from codes and practices that Abstraction was infinite. How could we communicate with Him? This Almighty of Great Nothingness? How could we make Him change the course of action already set in motion? Parameters of these immutable laws were pre-set. These were but the forces of nature, the

powers of the laws of physics operating in an infinite continuum of time eluding us of the very existence of God. There are no anti-matters yet that can break these parameters.

Good Karma always did not lead to good consequences, just as a good book always didn't come in the lime light of rave reviews. Such were the paradoxes of this life.

You were pregnant again Tahu Not with a love child but out of necessity For this was the only way you said you could be cured of your affliction No This child was not to happen Born still in your womb the Confidante called Pontu at the boot camp How well was his sleep How well did he eat and cope with life here But it was not working maa Pontu said He knew maa was sick he knew he could not provide for her Pael told me She told me every conversation she ever had with Pontu He was in trouble again The high counsellor deliberated He was picked up by authorities from the seas and brought here for training Hopelessness and optimism could not go hand in hand the Confidante tried to cheer him up He complied by saying he was okay He followed all the rules Going to gym classes to learn Kroll language played Do Do Hah ate and slept well He told maa that he never told them that he had been on the receiving end of bad behaviour from other riders They too were languishing here for days on We were all in the same boat struggling with the unfavourable waves of our times Maa he said that he had only just asked a mate how he was doing In a twisted reply he told him how did he think he was doing His mother was dying Shingdi had produced bumper crops this summer Harvest was really good Orchards were laden with mellow fruits the air was infused with smells of pineapples, guavas and pomegranates Ah that heavenly taste of ripened mango Oozing juices dripping over the hands of the little boys licking them over with tongues hanging out Ah I wish Shingdi really existed

Bittersweet. Milton wrote the magnificent Paradise Lost. Would there not be another Milton or a Shakespeare or James Joyce for the world to stoop before? Their enduring contributions, there was hardly a poet who had been loved so much, or an artist of this age. Perhaps, it was the entire unromantic society of today that was at fault. One that had failed to produce poets like Auden who would write those unforgettable words, 'the stars are not wanted now pack up the moon and dismantle the sun.' Regrettably, moirae of human race was seamlessly knitted into bullets, bayonets and canons; plight and intrigue. Today's world produced literature that only reflected this dismal set-up. What circumstances created riders that they were shunned? Only that they were but a product of a corrupt society. These boys, the riders didn't belong in the boot camp at Madura Island, but in a free world, a make belief world perhaps, called Shingdi.

Orange Soils

Nalia's brother's name was MD. He now lived in the land of Dravi, within a Jesuit house of God at Botany Bay. The priest of the parish was known as Paster Patrick. Since his friends deserted him for becoming a Jesuit, he could not live with them any longer; the good Paster took him on board and provided him with accommodation. It was an attic room at the top floor of the house of God. The room had been cleared and made into a bedroom with a single bed and a wooden table with a chair.

Two days after he moved in, MD received a phone call, as he lay in his bed one early morning. It was in fact from Pastor Patrick. He answered the phone excitedly. Pastor Patrick told him that he needed to speak with him urgently regarding his letter. MD was elated. He thought it was going to be good news. He had been expecting him to write this letter for some time now. Picking up the phone immediately, he told him that he was on his way down to his office.

Pastor Patrick was a kind, elderly man. He could have been a bit taller, but somehow it seemed his growth had been stunted by lack of nutrition. With rosary in his hand, he looked up at MD, as he entered the room. His rather long nose protruded unnaturally, between those keen small eyes. MD looked at him earnestly.

"I couldn't finish the letter," he said with a sheepish smile.

"Oh sorry, why not you finish?" MD asked.

"I'm afraid. I fell asleep. You need to find out when it's due."

"Okay, okay. Find out and me tell you tomorrow."

"How're your language lessons going?"

"Yes. Good, Sunday morning.

"Sunday mornings will change soon," Pastor Patrick said with a hangdog expression on his face. "From now on they'll be every Saturday morning."

"Why change?"

"There have been some changes within the house of God. Have you heard anything about your matter yet?"

"No. "

"How're you going?'

"No job. No money. You know? Really hard."

"I want to help you more, but my hands are tied."

"Thank you."

"You're very welcome. You're looking for a place to stay, right?"

"Yes, yes, I look every day."

"Let me know if you found something. Charity organisations would be another place to look for help. They organise finances for riders."

Pastor Patrick then consoled him, as he always did to all those down-trodden men and women, people who sought advice. These could be on various issues, inclusive of those relevant to riders. Some would come for solace in terminal illness. Others' could be lonesome, lost souls, who may not have fared well finding a grip in this world yet. These were foundlings, floating people not rooted in cause or destination.

Hopelessness or losing faith in God was not something he would encourage them to do; the same advice that he gave MD today. He told him to have faith in God. Something surely would happen soon. This uplifted his spirit. MD had confidence in Pastor Patrick's spirituality. If he prayed for him, then those prayers would be answered. In this firm belief, MD left him at that and stepped out on to the street hopeful that something surely would happen; if God deserted him, then there would be no other place to go. On television last night, he saw more *Blue Moon* boats on the furious sea. With every turn of those infinite waves, there seemed hope or hopelessness in the ebb and the flow. Where would they go? Where could they go? When he was crying in despair on the dirt road, where his parents had lost him on the border of the Southern Kingdom, people darted through in frantic desperation; someone had picked him up. Death was knocking on the door then, but he survived. He survived as a three-year-old. Who looked after him then? A guardian angel perhaps. He was too young to hope. Did he know what to hope for then? Yet, his fate led him into uncertainty and gave him a pathway which he had been following until now. He still hoped that a resolution would happen; he would get a permit card, perhaps even a permanent one, who knows? There was a God. There was a God when he was a follower of Mahammadan; there is God now that he had converted. God oversaw everyone. He was abstract; he could be shaped into any religion as one pleased. On the streets of Botany Bay, MD walked alone; as alone as he was on the fateful day, when he was left terrified on edge at three.

In the Parliament House, the parties debated every single day, whether or not riders should be given freedom in Draviland, the horrendous politics around it; Funding cuts were a regular event. Although there was no dearth of sympathy among many Dravidians, it had not yet crystallised. What was going to happen still hung in limbo.

Pontu in the meantime began to hallucinate in the boot camp awaiting an order of release. He started hearing voices, seeing visions and apparitions. They came and they went through his room like shadow. Officers at the facility or rather the body of psychologists and the Confidante consoled him in their caring, but prosaic words that he was much better here at the boot camp, because he didn't have to look for work, or accommodation in the community. People had no work rights either. He didn't have to worry about anything, buying food for instance. Stability. Do they call this stability? Being in jail? Had he not suffered enough in jails already in Mundip and in the Lost Winds? Not as posh perhaps, but this felt like punishment all the same. But he was able to escape and take the *Blue Moon* off the coast of Mundip. The boat sailed from a place that looked like some craggy hills in Mundip, if he didn't know better. There was a place to sleep in that little room in Mundip with 20 other riders jammed and locked up in that dingy room, with just a bottle of water and a small box of food for the whole day. Seven days in a row, after which the microbus brought them up here on a two hour drive to the boat. What was his future going to be? Uncertainty had almost killed him on the boat. How long would it take for the high counsellors to make a decision? How long a wait was this going to be? These were nervous questions that no one had answers for. Yet, the high counsellor sat in his office deliberating every day, while his mind delved deeper and deeper into the soggy soil of fertile but unrestrained imagination.

MD didn't have work rights. He wanted to work as volunteer, but not even that was allowed. Some of his other friends didn't have work rights either. But they found low paid work on strawberry farms for pittance a day, not even half the regular payment. Call it exploitation or whatever. But they secretly did this job, knowing that risks from tip-offs could result in severe punishments, cancellation of their permit cards, even being thrown back into the boot camp. Although MD abided by the law, he did not try to dob them in, as did other riders on the high counsellor's dob in line. It felt unnatural to do such a thing, although it could be legally or morally the right thing to do. Yet, in the name of solidarity, one just didn't do those things. From God's omniscient viewpoint, it didn't make much difference; no one stood any taller than the next boat-mate anyway. MD was an epitome of righteousness. He was only allowed to toil in community gardens and community kitchens which were within legal jurisdictions. He was on this way today to one such community kitchen, where they cooked Puntland food for the riders. He was not sure if he wanted to go. Neither was he sure if he would be welcome there. But he went any way. He took a bus from Botany Bay to Ashland on to Girudev Avenue. As he got off the bus, he found out that the place where the community kitchen was supposed to be held was closed. There wasn't going to be a party after all. He hung around in the park and thought about what else he could do today. Library was a good place, but he was there just yesterday; he dropped the idea.

MD put a finger over a scar on his hand and rubbed it. At ten, he went to religious school to study the great Book of Mohammadan. Nalia's father was a strict Mohammadan who decreed that this boy must attend religious studies every day. And he did. He repeated verses from the Book, not comprehending what he was reading. However, one day, when he asked his teacher, he was told that there was no need to *understand* the *Book*. God was happy to just see him read it. Caning was a regular practice from the teacher for asking the wrong questions.

"Hello," a gentleman just walked past with a grey fluffy poodle. MD smiled most graciously thinking how kind this gentleman was. What would it take for him to live in this country? The voluntary work at the house of Jesuit God, would that suffice? That was God's work! What else did he need to do to obtain a permanent permit? Pastor Patrick had once told him that if he were a brilliant writer or a soccer player, then the high counsellor would grant him a permit. He was none of those, although he could read and write in his first language. He could try his hand at soccer, he thought. What else was there? What about falling in love and getting married? But he shied away from the idea that he didn't even have enough to feed himself, let alone a wife. Pael would have made such a wonderful wife. He still had a fling for her. Pontu's little sister. The pretty little thing that he thought he was going to make his wife some day. How was Pontu now?

"No money, I not no m'money. Sorry, no Kroll," MD found himself talking and stammering to a mugger who just attacked him for money in the park.

"Turn your pockets, give me whatever you got in that wallet. 'Let me think. No wait'.

A man was robbing him. He wore a white rugby cap and a T-shirt with a pair of black denim shorts. There were several pockets in his shorts aligned in the front. Beard covered most of his face. MD's contemplation was suddenly broken. There was a situation here. He only had about 20 DR left from his fortnightly allowance from the Jesuit house of God. He took it out and gave it to him.

"Please not kill me, please. Only 20 DR."

MD was so close to the finish line, nearly there. He wasn't going to get killed now. The hustler grabbed the money unflinchingly without any intention of killing him and then he disappeared into thin air. Totally befuddled, MD managed to get up from the bench that he was sitting on somehow and made his way to the bus stop. Luckily, he had a bus pass which enabled him to make this trip. He sat down nervously on the first seat he saw; his hands were closed in a tight fist, as he kept looking out of the window. Next thing he knew was that he was at the door step of the Jesuit house. After the bus dropped him off, he went straight to see Pastor Patrick at his office at the back of the church. Pastor Patrick looked up at his lone figure standing grimly in the door way. He gave him the nod to come right in and signalled him with his hand to sit down on a chair opposite to the table. Before MD could speak, the Pastor started his speech.

"MD, there's something, I need to let you know," he said gravely.

"Yes Pastor. Tell me. Saturday coming I'm going to language class. Yes?"

"Oh, yes, yes; what I'm about to tell you though is something quite different," he said.

MD looked him curiously.

"There's a woman, who attends our house regularly. You might even know her. Her name is Angella."

"I know her not. "

"She is quite alone and could use a friend," he said in earnest. "She wishes to speak with you."

"Okay, Okay. News? Have any news for me?"

"No. Not yet, but I don't think a letter from me can help you?"

"Change religion. They kill me if go home."

"I understand that but you need to convince the high counsellor."

"Yes. Okay. Thank you."

"Was there anything else you wanted to say to me?"

"Yes, no."

"Okay then. Good luck."

MD left. He was dismayed. Within these doors of the house, he had been given temporary accommodation up in the attic. At the boot camp, pastors had come all the time to speak to them about the Jesuit religion to show them another way out of this harsh training environment. That was when he had met him and was introduced to the Jesuit religion. For all the faith that there was in the world, he felt strongly in that moment of desperation that Jesuit was the one to take him across to safety. He would be the one to not to fail him. Anxiety gripped him. He walked up to the window of the attic and looked downstairs. Cars and buses had lined up in a mad traffic rush in Botany Bay. One stream of cars deviated down the narrow slip lane like swarms of black ants breaking up in groups and moving away at different directions. Exactly the way men had fled the Lost Winds in groups formed by a sense of self organisation. They appeared from nowhere and yet everywhere. In one's and in two's they gathered as a crowd embarking on the *Blue Moon* heading for a journey of the unknown.

MD felt that one life, no one would even care, if it perished under those wheels; if he decided to jump. But that would defeat the purpose. He had come this far. He rushed into the toilet and threw up. He was beside himself. Looping in a dizzy spell, hallucinating, he staggered back and sat down on the edge of his bed. After that he knew nothing.

Needed to eat Prepared to sell meself A trade off with the wealthy farmer in Lost Winds Owed the farmer 50 thousand gold coins Was Nalia happy now She would stop talking I had become a Jesuit A knock on the door Lady stood outside door Smiled Kissed me fully on the lips What a beauty Dark beauty I took off with her. Oh the window was open last night. The harsh sun light just woke him up. What a lovely dream. What a pretty woman. MD smiled, as he went to brush his teeth. Pael would have been jealous. They could have been married by now, if it hadn't turned out like this. It had been foolish. No matter, one moved on; now that was a wise step. MD and those like him were children of the lesser gods. They were game to all those rulers running today's government; those authorities anywhere and everywhere all the way upto the edge of the four corners. Supremely more powerful and wealthy, they made decisions as to who were more expendable than the others based on their sterile rationalism, rather than sensitivity. Money and power gave society that right, exposing humans into an ever growing, ever expanding asymmetrical society of exploitation.

Small people like MD were no match to the cunning and the powerful. Less did they care about their ambitions and how they could get ahead in life. Whatever window of opportunity was open to the disenfranchised, they took advantage of it anyway they could. Religion didn't do much for them. It didn't mellow the mighty in any way to help unhinge a door for their easy access to fortune. Conversely, it appeared that God only worked mysteriously for the rich and the powerful. That they always profited in the favourable winds, and continually made a killing.

It was time to have breakfast. MD walked along the streets and thought that last night's episode should not have happened. At any rate it should not recur. There was no room here for the feeble hearted and the meek. He was going to get some bread from the grocery store and milk just down the road. 20 DR were taken from him yesterday, and he only had just ten to get him through the week until his next payment came through. He was returning with a bag and met his friend *Blue Moon* number 998. Both had come on the same boat and literally were on the same boat as well. He smiled at MD and he smiled back at him. It seemed that the man had started work in this shop. They stopped to exchange a few words in their own language.

"How're you?"

"I'm good and you?"

"I'm good too."

"Has Jesuit religion done anything for you yet?"

"Not yet. But I do believe that it would."

"You live in a fool's paradise. You need to engage lawyers, not Jesuits."

"God gives me strength and motivation. Where would I be without him today?"

"Which One? Mohammadan or Jesuit? Who saved you the last time?"

"I don't know. But I still live and that's a miracle. I'm thankful to the one God. Call it what you must. And I'm not going to give up on Him.

"Go on believing in whatever. No God can save you now. We have reached our journey's end. They're sending us back. Don't you hear the news anymore? They hate us. Dravidians want us out. State will find some ways to send us back."

"What're you talking about?"

"You don't know? Unless the high counsellor believes that you're a real rider there's no way, they'll let you stay. Just telling them you will be killed is not enough. You need to show evidence, papers. Do you have any?"

"No. What would you do if they told you that you couldn't live here anymore? What would you do?" MD asked flustered.

"I would get into language classes, a course which would let me stay here, find proper government lawyers. Supply documents." 998 answered confidently.

"You're so naive. If God can't help who would? Your lessons would? Your permit processing lawyers?"

"That's what I think?"

"Our pathways are different surely. Let's not go down that path where one has to expel God. One could get lucky too, you know?" MD said stubbornly.

"Try everything. Who knows what will work in the end. Who knows?" said 998 despondently. MD left him there at the crossroads. What horrible plight. He looked at all the pretty girls in pigtails and tights but quickly moved his vision, as though it were a crime to even look at them. It was better that he didn't get into those things, better to keep out of trouble. Who knows what would lead to what? He returned to his room in the attic of his abode. Who had more power? God or a permit processing human? He poured himself a glass of milk and sat down on his single bed donated by charities. One didn't need to have that much furniture. That would be indulgence and greed. His beloved prophet was a carpenter. He lived frugally, so did MD. Prophets did have a lot to teach, if only one would stop to listen. Less was more in their judgement in which the life of the mind was paramount. Even atheists could use some frugality. Greed and corruption were being justified today, in the name of what? Progress and modernity? One didn't even have to go that far. Happiness was nearly a thing of the past and so was innocence; the last unicorns lingered in the shadows, before they completely disappeared. Excessive power was corrupting. It made people forget what golden mean was.

MD took out a slice of bread and put it on a saucer. Sun lights streamed through the small wooden attic window picture framed in white. He tore up the slices in little pieces and dipped each of them into milk with his smooth chocolatey index finger and thumb before he put them in his mouth; bread, he dipped in the water, a man of tenacity and patience, such virtues would be rewarded surely but slowly. His cheap canvas sneakers were still on his feet. A toe was beginning to peek through a hole. No need to buy another pair, just yet. These would do fine. For a while at least, he decided. The news was on. Every single day, it was the same. Oh turn the boats away, turn them away. Riders were not welcome here. Yet, some people's hearts said differently, as they took to the streets for rallies and demonstrations. What crimes had the riders committed though? Being poor. Was that a crime? Were proper avenues open only to those who had clout and money? Queue jumpers, what other pathways were available for the poor? Again, he was looping.

Hingyans were fleeing in great haste from the Southern Seas. Authorities there were chasing them out of the country. The little boy suddenly fell down from his mother's lap. These were multitude of noises of scurried feet; feet almost trampling the three year old. Some didn't have any shoes at all; others had dusty and grimy, torn old sandals on. The cries of the petrified boy were nearly buried in those sounds. Like a herd of frightful giraffe chased by the mighty lion, they ran. In a sweep, someone picked him up. Off they went again and entered safe haven in relief. This little thing, this earthling was then left on the sideway of a river bank. Hunger and thirst nearly killed him. But he was picked up yet once again and given a full life this time. He grew up and 15 years later, he was told about this flight, but his parents could not be found anywhere. 'Did they ever look for me?' MD wondered, for he had become the emblematic stray of the moor.

People behaved strangely when they were pushed like that. Motherly affections, all those fondles' didn't count suddenly. Nothing came before the 'I' factor. Me. Save myself first, transforming in some kind of an alter-ego grey area of existence. But in a moment like this, those were decisions people made. These moments brought out the worst in them. 'Mother, did you even realise that you dropped me?' 'Did you grieve for me later?' 'One day, mother, I would like to find you and bring you here.' 'How was I going to pay back 50 thousand gold coins? Pael and I could have been married and lived in the city. I could have worked on construction site. But bad things happened in the slums too when parties from the regime came along to recruit, when all we ever wanted was to be neutral and peaceful. They would have abducted Pael, as they did to so many others in the city. Aggrieved people still looked for their sisters and their mothers. MD's thoughts were rapid and changeable. He flipped from one issue to the next. Relative safety was guaranteed here perhaps, but milk, bread or honey, whatever they said flowed here certainly wasn't true. He must look for accommodation. There wouldn't be much left after paying rent from his monthly allowance. Jesuits would find something for him and he was sure of that. This was not just a house of God, but also a house of welcome.

White Vines

"You must be MD," Angella said after the sermons one Sunday morning, as MD was just about to leave.

"Yes, I MD."

"Pastor Patrick told me so much about you. Are you still looking for accommodation?"

"Yes, very hard, expensive room."

"Do you mean it's expensive to rent a house?"

"Yes, yes."

"Look, I have an extra room in my house. And I'm quite happy to have you as a boarder. Pastor Patrick told me much about you. You could move in anytime you're ready."

"Thank you." "

"You can pay me if you like, or whatever, you want to. I just wanted to say that you're welcome."

"Thank you. I ask Pastor Patrick, then you tell I."

"Sure, any time."

MD was exuberant. He couldn't express his gratitude as much as he wanted to because of the lack of language competence, which still followed the linguistic parameter of his first language, replaced by the target words only. A complete transition into Dravi Kroll had not occurred yet. He considered this lady thoughtfully.

The appearance of Angella in his life was enchanting. Zeus, himself must have sent this person to him in a moment of impulsive munificence. He could not wait to tell this to Pastor Patrick and could not wait to get his stuff out from the attic room. Why though would this middle-aged lady who could very well be his aunt's age want a companion? Whatever, young or old, he was eager to go. MD was 25 and judging by her wrinkles and hollow cheeks, she looked at least 50. But then, he could be wrong. Judging anyone was not something he wanted to do, let alone their age. Age, wasn't a factor.

"When come I?"

"Yes, yes come around anytime. The room's yours."

Angella left him rather flippantly, as she collected her black dated bag and walked out of the pew.

"Oh yes, and get the address from father Patrick, would you?"

MD looked at her, a bit baffled. He was spectacularly candid and pure; his thin, soft lips, slightly apart. He did not follow her, but turned around on his heels and went straight towards the office to speak to Pastor Patrick. His prayers had been answered after all. He wore the same white cotton shirt today and the same over sized brown pants, picked up from the house of God's second hand shop. Through the holes of his sneakers, the toe still showed which he tried to hide. The lady on the contrary attempted to cover none of her grey hair, which was cut really short, as though, she was growing it back from a shaven head.

73

Only too glad to be accepted, MD didn't know her situation and couldn't care less. Surely, there was going to be a change; he just knew it.

Pastor Patrick knew he was going to come so he waited for MD in his office. As soon as he entered, he looked up and smiled.

"Did you speak with Angella? What did she say?"

"Yes. I go her house."

"When do you want to leave?"

"I leave morning tomorrow, yes?"

"Okay. She is a nice lady. Both of you can come to the house of God together."

"Thank you."

"Anytime."

MD couldn't contain his excitement. He jumped a few steps ahead to his attic room and opened the door. Closing it behind him, his gaze fell on the school bag that he carried to his Kroll language classes, a blue ordinary back pack. This was a nearly empty room, with just a black fleecy jumper and a pair of black pants placed on the foot rest of his bed; on one corner of the room, sat his bag pack. He opened the zipper in a real hurry, clumped his clothes together and began to put them in the bag along with his books and pen. Of all his possessions, the one thing that was most precious to him was the Jesuit Book that he read every day. Carefully, he put that into the bag too. Freedom was imminent. However, when he thought of the lady, he wondered if she was doing this out of kindness or was there something else, an ulterior motive that he couldn't understand - He tried not to think about it, he was happy that he was not homeless.

That day seemed to pass slowly. Anxiously, he walked up to the window and looked outside. How amazing the city looked today. Jacarandas were in bloom just across the house. Synchronised in the calming winds, the fall of the delicate petals' on the street of Botany Bay stirred symphony in the mind. He was glad that he decided to live, not get crushed under those horrible big wheels. Pastor Patrick was his only companion so far and now this new lady that had come to aid. There was some progress in his otherwise stalemated situation. An opportune moment was about to break through.

"Mother, why do people like fighting so much?"

The perceptive child MD had asked his adopted mother once, as he sat by her on their front yard. His mother had just kindled a nice fire to boil a pot of potatoes. He was helping her with the wash and putting the clothes out on the line. A crow sat on the clothes. He picked up a pebble from the dirt floor and threw at it. In no time its faeces would be all over the wash. His mother smiled, blowing through a pipe to get the fire going into the clay stove.

"Because, it's just something they must do."

"Why can't people live peacefully? Why do they must go to war?"

"Because, they're greedy. They want more and more."

"Enough is enough. They should all stop fighting and start farming."

His mother had laughed at that.

"What's farming got to do with anything?"

"That's the most important thing. Isn't it? Food. I hate being hungry."

"Is that what you want to become when you grow up?"

"Maybe, but I also want to go to school. I like school. I like nursery rhymes."

"Run along now. Go play with your sister, you've done enough chores for one day."

Nalia and he had played hopscotch near their mother as she called them for lunch later. It was a simple meal of mashed potato and rice, which they had on the floor mat. Father had joined later. Life was simple then, but he was happy. Why did it all have to change? MD turned away from the window. He could still remember his mother in a red and black cotton check garb. She always kept her head covered with the fallen piece of the scarf over the shoulder. Nalia also had the same type of untailored, flowing garb wrapped around her. There was so

76

much love that the thoughts welled up tears to his eyes now. Paster Patrick loved him too and he loved him back, perhaps not as much as he loved his own father but close. The love card was played. Pael had told him once, as they were growing up that she wanted him as a husband. He had laughed and said.

"I have no money. How would I buy you bangles? What would we eat?"

"I don't need bangles. I want you. We will grow our own food."

"We need a farm for that. Where's the land? Who'll give us land?"

"Good question," she said and left it at that.

MD wondered what she was doing now. Her brother Pontu had left the village the last time he spoke to them before MD's conversion into Jesuit. That was a little while ago. Pael must be worried sick, thinking about Pontu. 'Where was he? Was he here in Dravi or in Madura Island? Where was Pontu?' He whispered to himself. Were they ever going to see each other again, in this lifetime? Then he had to think of his new religion, the new life that he was about to begin. Pontu might not be too happy about it. He let the thoughts slip away; he let Pael slip away.

MD brushed his hair in the bathroom and looked at himself in the mirror. Might not be a terribly handsome man, but he wasn't such a bad looking bloke either. A thin smile appeared on his lips, as he packed his tooth brush, paste and shaving materials. There was a tiny cake of runny soap leftover in the shower. He packed that too. Then he made his bed; well, he would have to sleep in it tonight. If he had work rights today, he could have sent some money back to Nalia, mother and father. He could have given them a better life there. Father could have bought some land, Nalia and mother could've started a business. But then, people from political parties would have come around and wrecked it. He was running away because of this debt and it was going to get older and older. MD would have been condemned to a lifetime of slave labour, labour without pay which was the trade off. He would never really have settled the score; hence, he would never really have the time for paid jobs. Even if he did have paid work on construction site, could he ever save so much to payback? What an astronomical amount of money? At least for him; it was an equivalent of 5000 in Dravi currency.

Seasons came and seasons went. Spring would shower its divine beauty into the world, but his life would be a slog and pass by without taking pleasure in it. A knock on the door startled him. He opened it and Pastor Patrick was there, standing peacefully with his rosary dangling through his fingers.

78

"Hello MD. I wondered if you wanted to join me for dinner tonight. Since, I might not be able to say good bye to you tomorrow."

"Sure, sure. Thank you," MD smiled happily.

Pastor Patrick took a quick glimpse at the neat room. For an old fashioned room, it was quite a pretty nook. It didn't look dilapidated and MD collected no rubbish. Walls were white as the driven snow without a single scoff mark around the edges of either the window sill or the door knob. MD would make a good tenant. Any room he rented would be a reflection of his soul.

This house of God only reinforced in him what he had already cherished; kindness, consideration for others and frugality. In all honesty, he hoped to pay the farmer back the money that he had borrowed impulsively. What role theology exactly played in his life in shaping his character was yet unknown, apart from the solace he derived just from regular attendance at the house of God.

Conversion had no greater influence on anything than being an ordinary atheist or a heathen. Be it a Mohammadan or a Jesuit, it was yet just another religion, no more or less anointed, than the pagan believers in the temple of Athena. Religion did not feed people no more than it had during paganism. What charms did faith hold over people that it blinded them to reason? Drove them crazy? Crazy enough to kill mates and break well bonded relationships.

Faith was unbelievably more powerful than state laws. Fear of God, afterlife, hell, heaven and purgatory were but revisitations from ancient pagan order. Spiritualism, philosophy, theology were out of reach for most people. Most people couldn't even begin to conceive what these meant. God conceptualised in his or her image, a decidedly human image was the extent of their understanding of God. Evolution had not really liberated or united them to pursue a belief of the one, great Nothingness; on the contrary, it had shackled them ever more strongly to many irreconcilable belief systems.

It was six 'o' clock. Dinnertime. MD joined Pastor Patrick in his dining room. The table was set for two. The Pastor served himself and him two bowls of mushroom soup and bread. Pleased with MD's politeness and mannerisms, he was sure that he would gradually develop friendship with MD. He was slowly turning into a good Jesuit. There weren't that many issues to discuss tonight because of his limitation with the language, but this conversation showed his sensitivity and intelligence.

"I hope you like the new place."

"Yes, yes, I come to this house for language class."

"Yes, she will bring you here."

"I read great Book morning time."

"If you had work permit, what would you want to become?"

"I people help maybe," he laughed unsure of himself.

"And how would you do that?"

"Money sent to my father home."

"What about yourself? You'll need money to get married one day?"

"I still not forget Nalia, mother and father. And Pael."

"Have they not stopped talking to you?"

MD lowered his head quietly and continued to stir his soup. In his resilience, he believed that one day they would understand this decision. Besides, they knew as much as he did that they were not his biological family. Perhaps this conversion wouldn't hurt them that much. That was what the instinct said anyway. However, he could not explain all this to the father, but the good priest knew how much love there still was. He had not become completely embittered after all. His life's journey, as onerous as it maybe, had not made him completely soulless. And that was always a good sign. Dinner was over and MD said his good byes, promising to meet him every Sunday for mass. Pastor Patrick smiled mysteriously and gave him Angella's address.

Tomorrow's adventure held enigma for him. He kept awake imagining what this place was likely to be. He wanted sleep in order to prepare himself for the two hour bus ride from Botany Bay to the West Mountains. He had pain in his stomach at the prospect of meeting Angella the next day. In the morning MD set off yet again for the unknown. He looked around the room that he had grown to like and down the window one last time. Quietly, he opened the door to not to make too much noise. In the same pants that he had on yesterday, white T-shirt and torn canvas shoes, he left the church and closed the door firmly behind him. He walked up to the bus stop and waited for the right bus. The bus numbers were written for him on a piece of paper, and given to him last night by Pastor Patrick.

With the back pack tight on his shoulders, he sat down like a stooped turtle on the bench. People gathered in twos and threes; all waiting for the same bus, heading towards a common destination. Hardly, anyone spoke to him or each other for that matter; they measured him up top to toe and moved a tad further away, creating a bigger gap. MD felt awkward, but continued to wait patiently. His mobile rang suddenly and Angella's name appeared on the screen.

"Hello," MD answered with a smile.

"You, on the bus yet?"

"No bus coming, I wait."

"It's late."

And then the bus was seen in the horizon.

"Yes, yes! Coming bus,"

"Oh okay, see you soon. Have a nice trip. And yes, I'll pick you up from the bus-stop here. "Okay?"

"Okay. See you."

MD boarded the bus with the others and handed the ticket that Pastor Patrick bought for him; a one way ticket to the West Mountains. He took a window seat and sat down feeling a strange warmth and confidence. He looked up to see that every other passenger avoided sitting beside him. On the empty seat he put his back pack down. Only last night he had a shower just before dinner, so there was nothing unclean about him. His looks were good and shaven. Anyway, he didn't want to dig further into it. Looking out of the window, he saw the city wake up to the smell of coffee. The brilliant Poinciana trees were a blaze of colours in the calm morning. The bus rolled on. Apart from the driver looking occasionally through the rear view mirror, nothing too dramatic happened. Most people in the bus avoided eye contact; he did the same, as he drifted off.

What was Pael doing now? Was she sitting down in her yard with her cascading black hair lying across the floor of her small house like black velvet carpet? She was probably combing it in a long serpentine braid and then tying it up with a red ribbon at the tail. She was putting on her matching red bangles too; one after another with utmost care so they didn't break. Mother, Father and Nalia, what were they up to? Who knows? Maybe he shouldn't think of them anymore. Block the thoughts, he told himself. Block all thoughts. Think of nothing at all just blankness; totally blank; yet the mind thought of the attic room, the cars on the road through the little window and the Jacarandas. Cabbages, Cauliflowers' and Zucchini, turned out pretty good in the community garden this season; they would last a while before the next crop was out. 998's permit maker or his migration agent had probably done wonders for him by now, if he was not mistaken. Could anyone change the pathway that one was meant to be on, regardless of what faith one followed? The little pesky voice kept talking endlessly. Confidence was deceptive sometimes, egging people on to an end with catastrophic consequences. Success though was just incidental on the flipside. Results were never guaranteed neither was the planning of right or wrong, good or bad. Man proposed and God disposed, the much clichéd phrase was the ever diabolical dilemma of the human mind. Oh, he must try and sleep a little. Wavering in the bus, he slowly dozed off. Half consciously, he knew that the bus had stopped and started to take new passengers on-board. Some read a book; others nodded off like him or simply gazed out of the window.

Purple Waves

"I want to be with babu. You've reached in nadir of that river," Tahu lamented in Nalia's mother's house in the village one day.

"Those pills? Do they not work? You've been on them for many days now," commented Nalia.

"I see him. I hear his voice. He comes and goes through my room like a shadow, accusing me of casting him into the river. But he was blue, blue as stonefish spikes. He just didn't breathe; pills don't work; one blue and white or pink, oh! I don't know. At least he has stopped beating me now; oh! How he beat me every single night in drunkenness; yes, for money and to sleep with him."

Tahu sat on the front yard of Nalia's mother's house with her legs stretched out and entwined at the feet. She looked not at Nalia or her mother but out into oblivion.

"That night of the big storm, I came home from work. There he was sitting on the bed drunk. I was pregnant with babu. He asked to see my purse I did not give it to him. I was tired. Oh, so tired from a whole day of stitches in the factory that it gave stiches in my tummy."

Tahu stopped and took a deep breath. Nalia's mother made some tea on the small wood stove in the front yard. The flimsy aluminium kettle hissed, as it blew some vapours out. Nalia brought two little cups made of clay and set them down on the floor of the yard on the sitting mat where they talked. Nalia's mother poured out three cups of tea already made in the kettle with fresh cow's milk and molasses. Nalia handed a cup to her and took one for her. A shiny big raven came from nowhere and sat on the cane fence under the over-extended branches of the mango grove. Holding the cup of tea in one hand, Nalia stood up and tried to get rid of the raven.

"Pills not working. Then when I didn't give him the purse, he slapped me hard on the face, so hard that I fell down. I howled with pain. Yes. I did."

Tahu shook her head, her gaze transfixed on the floor, as though she were talking to nobody else but herself. She wore a long garb of black checks. She couldn't care less if it covered her bosom. Parts of it slipped off her shoulder. Her hair was undone. Nalia took a comb and put it to work gently pushing its teeth all the way to those roots, and down to her black knotted hair ends. She untangled the knots slightly running her fingers through. Tea was getting cold.

"C'mon finish your tea, now," said Nalia's mother.

"I need to go home. I'll take the evening boat. He stopped beating me for a while, after I lost babu," Tahu said picking up her tea. "Babu was doing well, and then one day he just breathed no more. I ran like crazy to the doctor, they said he

86

was gone. Gone. Yes, never see babu again. Never. I brought him to the bank of river Murma and took a boat. Storm loomed in the sky, the boat whirled around on the big waves; there was darkness everywhere. So frightening. I couldn't care less. I tried, tried to wake him up in my lap, offered him milk, but he slept the sleep of a lifetime. And in that moment of panic, I started to cry and lowered him to the foaming waves; gave him to Murma. Murma will take care of him, right? I know, he told me, he smiled. Babu. Babu. Where's babu? Bring Babu."

Tahu's eyes popped out large, as she wailed and shrieked reaching the limitlessness of the sky. Raven flew away nervously and Nalia with her mother continued to gape at her in despair. Helplessness was one thing but what just happened now was boundless misery.

Yet, Nalia's wheel of fortune kept turning. In our random fate-ridden existence, every one supposedly had a fair go. She saved a fair bit of money from her job working as a domestic helper. There was a deathly shadow in that house too; but she decided to give the money to her mother to buy another milk cow in the village. Courage had never left her side, even at her lowest. As they sat there with Tahu, Nalia's father rushed in.

"What's wrong?"asked Nalia's mother frantically.

"Something's happened next door."

"What? Is Pontu's father in trouble? Is Pontu in trouble again?"

"I don't know but Miah is on his way to the police station."

"Oh? Why is that?"

"He said to me in a small voice that police had been asked by the regime to investigate Pontu's case in the village."

"What for? Hasn't enough happened already?"

"I don't know."

Tahu raised herself suddenly, and said she wanted to nap. Nalia took her to the room and made her a bed on the floor caringly, with a patched up sheet looking like seven colours of the rainbow. Tahu lay down quietly, stricken with grief. Nalia embraced her tenderly and kissed her oily dishevelled hair. Tahu smiled wanly and lay down closing her eyes quietly whispering almost chanting, 'Babu says come come maa come to me He stretches arms Little arms Baby fingers stretches them as far as they would go Babu is leaving wait wait for me Dont go just yet Babu no no no...medicine no dont work...the city He remarried.

Nalia left her to her half-formed thoughts, as she came out to sit with her parents.

"Miah was interrogated by the police. They asked him if he knew where his nephew was on the night of the murder."

"What did he say?"

"That he was asleep. I believe the people from the autocratic party killed him. That nephew had made many enemies you see. That's why they killed him and made Pontu the scapegoat. Police, the head magistrate, everyone is in on it. That's what I think."

"Mmm. Will they find the killer? Pontu will not be able to return until then. Police will throw him in jail," sighed Nalia's mother.

"Anyway, Nalia's mother, give me some tea,"

"In a while, rice is nearly done; I'm also going to fry some salted fish Nalia brought from the city."

Overall the family looked much healthier for Nalia's earnings. All she needed now was clemency from the village elders for her rape. It was an ironical situation. She needed their sympathy, not rebuke.

"Mohammad has become a Jesuit and changed his name to MD, hasn't he? Don't give me the phone when he calls."Nalia's father said. "I raised him like my own."

Nalia stood by listening away. She jumped in that very moment saying,

"He should stay wherever he is father. They might kill him, if he tried to come."

"Who would?" asked Nalia's mother.

"Oh, don't be so naive, mother. Jesuit or no Jesuit, if he's happy, then let him be. It's not our place to make a decision."

"No? Where would he be today if I hadn't found him crawling at the ferry stop?"

"I don't know. It's his life. You have given him a loving home father; fed him when even we didn't have enough to eat ourselves. Let it go. You've done your bit."

Nalia's father kept quiet. Her mother put the rice down on the paved floor with boiled potatoes and some home grown fresh spinach in it that she had plucked earlier from the small, vegetable patch by the house. She made another cup of tea for father.

"You're probably right. I won't mull over it anymore. Certainly won't give the wicked farmer the sadistic joy of losing him; the hard slog that the bastard was going to put him through."

"Anyway, wake Tahu up. Lunch is nearly ready," said Nalia's mother.

It was beginning to get late in the afternoon. On the edge of the earth, the sun slowly diminished. An unexpected calmness dropped in the atmosphere. In one short life, this drama would end. And that would be the end of it all; those, who suffered the worst, were the ones most deluded by the notion that this life was forever. Oh, how calm? How peacefully the river Murma flowed today? A mere twitter of a bird in the heavy groves, the shepherd's distant tune caught in the flute wafted through the

90

air. There appeared to be no grimy crimes threatening such delightful sensations of undulated serenity.

Tahu woke up. She said she was hungry and that sleep had made her feel so much better. She needed to be back in the village away from that horrible monster; enjoy the tranquillity of the river Murma, to be closer to her Babu. Babu needed her to be alive, so he could make his regular visitations, so she would see her baby smiles that emerged a hundred times on the mouth of his un-toothed gum. As they sat down to eat, there was sound of a motorbike revving up just outside the hut.

"Nalia's father, do you want to check who that might be?" asked her mother.

He stood up and walked to the fence. Two men on a motorbike had come to talk business with him. Nalia, Tahu and her mother stayed indoors and listened pale-faced as he argued with the men.

"Either join us, our resistance party, or you pay heavily," they threatened.

"Resistance party? I'm not into politics. I don't want to be a part of what you do.

"And what do you think we do?"

"I don't know; killing, looting, and rallying, all in a day's work."

"Is that what you think? Have you forgotten MD's debt of 50 thousand gold coins, he borrowed from the farmer?"

And then heavy sounds of punching followed by a terrified bawl.
"Aww, Oh God! Oh! My nose, nose. I'm done. These men have killed me."

"We haven't even started yet," they scorned. "We'll come back next month, make sure you've 10 thousand ready for us. Or else, we'll knock the living day lights out of you."

"Please, I'm a poor man. There's no money. We go hungry most of the time. How can we pay what you demand?"

"We don't want to know. We will be back in a month's time. Keep the money ready."

Saying so, they got back on the motorbike and disappeared along the dirt path. Nalia's father appeared in a moment with a frightening nose bleed. He flopped down on the mat and held his head down supporting it on his palms. Surely, they were the wealthy farmer's men. Indeed they were his hit-men.

"Oh, good God. Nalia, bring the pitcher of water from that corner and give him a wash."

Nalia and Tahu dabbed his nose with a damp cloth.

This was a common occurrence in the village. People came regularly to recruit apolitical and peaceful village folks to join demonstrations and rallies. Make them do all the dirty work. They were tormented and threatened into subjugation. Like a great domino falling, those who felt unsafe and could find passage took the risk of leaving the village showing up in another part of the world. Terrible crimes against, men, women and children were being committed in the name of resistance against an autocratic regime to stabilize democracy. Now that was an irony indeed. Nalia's father frowned. He couldn't think anymore. Nalia suggested, sell the milk cow. Their only source of sustenance came from selling milk in the market. This had to happen this very moment? When things were beginning to look up a bit?

"They will be back. This is what has happened to Miah too, before his nephew was killed. They came back, again and again for more gold coins until they milked him dry," he sighed and spoke meekly.

"Wasn't it enough that his nephew got killed? Well, you can't stay here," Nalia declared.

"Where could we go?"

"I'll think of something."

"What? What will you think of? There's nothing remaining besides death."

"No. It doesn't have to end like that. You're coming to the city with me."

"Are you out of your mind? What would I do there?"

"Whatever; pull people carriages; live in a slum."

None of her parents quite warmed up to the idea of being dispossessed in this manner. But then what else could they do? Anything was better than dying in the hands of these extortionists. MD would have been either worked to death or killed by now by the rich farmer and his powerful men if he had stayed. In a moment, the situation changed. What seemed like a peaceful afternoon, turned dramatically to this. These were changeable circumstances, which swung wildly like a busted clock pendulum.

"Shall we eat? I must seek help. Nalia has Mohammad called yet? Mundip. The Transporters," Nalia's father thought aloud.

Raven came back with a big caw and swooped down, to pick up some salted fish off one of the plates with his pointed, black beak. The rice went cold. Steadily, with fish at the tip of the long beak, he frisked about and sat down on the fence. 'Caw, caw' he ate it fast, seemed to say 'you're in a losing battle, join'em, leave'em, there's no escape. It was 'Nemesis', howled the chorus of Sophocles of Oedipus Rex. What act of hubris was this? No more or less than what Oedipus had committed? Naught a Rex by a long shot, but Nalia's father succumbed to ill fate just the same.

Nalia's mother set out the plates again and gave each some food. Tahu must go home to her aunt's next door. She, who

94

raised her after her mother had passed away in the last great storm. She left them in dismay. There wasn't a single family in the Lost Winds, except for the influential, which enjoyed some peace here. Each had their own burden of woes, transpiring in their own way into classic tragedy. The graver a situation became, however, the more people hung in the balance, and the more astute they became. Shingdi was a far cry, the ideal world that was out of reach. They learnt to survive on the edge, avoid bullets, and lie with confidence. In a way, they created a wall of deception to give them protection; a kind of immunity behind which the underprivileged hid. Somehow, the lies of the less fortunate were deemed as more horrifying in the eyes of the law than corporate bullying or political transgression.

In the cover of darkness, Nalia and her family set off and disappeared, with their two milk cows. A month later, when those two terrorists came back to extort money, they found that the house had become a property of that wealthy and powerful farmer that who acquired it as a trade off to MD's debt of 50 thousand. It was a real bargain, because the land itself would have cost over two hundred thousand. With the house, it would have been much more. Undoubtedly, those two men were hired assassins of the wealthy farmer.

One evening, Tahu sat by the river Murma, talking and smiling to her baby. The world thought she had become completely mad. However, they could not see what she saw in her madness, as she rambled on. She told her baby that she wondered where Nalia went, without so much as a word, 'she simply disappeared into thin air babu; no letter; no phone calls; no nothing.' And then she smiled sweetly looking over the river as though the apparition stood on the contours of the sparkled water and smiled back. 'She is? You think she is well? Whatever happened to those two milk-cows? Oh. My God, Now that's clever. She took advantage of their vulnerability? Their daughter was quite dead, wasn't she?'

Nalia was able to negotiate with her employer and his wife into taking her parents in and to make a cow-shed for the cows. They sold fresh milk, a rarity in the city of Grosnii, to every house hold that they could possibly reach through Nalia's employer. In return, they supplied free milk to them, a trade off for a nice bedroom that they got in the big house.

The apparition seemed to be telling her all this and Tahu was seen laughing her head off, still looking towards the river Murma. She stretched her hand and brought it close to her chest in a gesture of hugging and then protruding her mouth towards emptiness in the way of kissing. The village boys who saw her called her insane, but she sure had a method in her madness, which only she and her baby understood. They communicated every day. She would leave her house, at his beck and call. 'Nalia, if I find those men I shall most certainly kill them and throw their bodies in the river Murma. No one will know it was me, because I don't exist for most people. My insanity will be my alibi and my defence Nalia. I swear I would kill them next time I saw them. This much I owed you my dear friend. Babu and I would do this together. We put a curse on them, as I did on that brute of a husband of mine. Where was he now? Do you know anything about him? He must be dead. Cold dead by now for certain. Wail. I wail Nalia, I know not why, I'll be one with Babu soon. We're one in spirit as close as one possibly can be with the dead. Dead? Who said, he's dead. He's just as alive as anyone else. You will see Nalia how those two die. You will read it in the paper one day. What do you care? You never even bothered to tell me where you were. Babu knows best and he told me. Wait until I finish the job at hand. We would have so much fun killing those two. They deserved nothing better; God knows they didn't.'

About the same time, Nalia felt a strange tug in her heart too, as she sat in the cow shed milking the cows. 'Tahu, I now milk the cow everyday; your black locks must be spread out on the silver river Murma when you bathe in it; do you think about me too? Look for me? All those times we spent together. Tahu, your husband was found dead in the corner of the alley. There was a fire and he was too drunk to run; he died from smoke inhalation. Fool, I've been such a fool. I didn't get in touch with you.' Surely enough, the newspapers in the city read that two people on a motorbike were driving past the river Murma at dusk one day. They fell into a trap of a fishing net thrown out from the blue. The net got entangled around them and the men were dragged off the stalling motorbike while they were still alive; and then straight into the water at high afternoon tide. All this happened pretty fast, before they could escape. The bodies slowly sunk into the depths of the river.

Such was the sorrowful fate of these two blokes. A convoluted contraption was pulled up the next day, as cold as fish laid over night on the virgin snow.

Gold Foliage

Pontu sat very quietly in his room at Madura Island boot camp where he was undergoing mandatory military training. Dravi authorities wanted to fully ensure that riders received it. Conscription was frequent in Draviland as they were in perpetual war with the neighbouring state of Zelda. Being educated on Draviland laws and social values was another important aspect before gaining freedom of release. More importantly, they had to make sure that riders did not pose a threat to the citizens of Dravi.

Smoking guns filled up the atmosphere around him suddenly. One man just died here a couple of hours ago. This man wanted freedom so badly that he wanted to flee. This was considered mutiny. Where no guns were even supposed to be brought in, let alone be used, as trainees didn't carry guns, guards shot him and killed him. They were always unarmed. Fear never left Pontu's side. He hid himself with 20 others cramped under a bed. He felt he would get caught in the cross fire and lose his life too. He thought of maa but had not called her.

The last time he spoke to her, she was too upset to carry on a conversation. It saddened him too; he had then decided not to call her again. He wanted to send money home. Feeling quite useless, he didn't think it was going to be so hard to earn money or to make a living here. Dangerous as it was, no escape was actually possible from this place unless they volunteered to be returned. The ubiquitous presence of the sea being just one problem, the overall law and order situation was another concern. People came here to escape persecution, but he felt that this was a different kind of a trap. What was more of a horror was that riders became suicidal just from sheer uncertainty. Sleeping pills didn't help and it was just as futile as it was to see psychologists generally known as *Confidantes* in this boot camp. Repeated monotonous questions shot from them, gave Pontu no peace of mind at all; on the contrary, made him angry. Hell begot hellish behaviour and that was certain. Riders who came from other remote parts of this two-moon planet gave him suggestive looks. They even invited him to come into their room at night. Pontu was still a child, not quite an adult yet. At 17, he didn't want to lose his optimism; neither did he want to be raped by other trainees. After all, he survived the formidable Mundip forests by remaining hidden for days on end from the police there. One day he went to see his Confidante to put things in perspective.

"Optimism is a good thing," the Confidante said.

"Yes, I'm not suicidal. Not yet. But it scares the hell out of me, when I hear others are. I've seen on TV how people kill themselves here because they got tired of waiting."

"Yeah, I know waiting can be a tiresome thing, the worst that there is."

"Is there nothing you or anyone could do? Everyone tells me to be patient; investigations are underway. Has anyone been to see my father yet? What's taking them so long to complete background checks? I haven't killed anyone. I was framed; they set me up.

"I know, but you know what? There's always light at end of the tunnel. You just need to wait it out."

"And I am, of course, that's all we do, isn't it? Wait and be patient, while maa suffers. I don't call them anymore. It upsets me to see her so sad. She cries endlessly on the phone."

"What do you do, when she does that?"

"I try to console her. Well, used to, but I feel I'm in a losing battle. Words dry up in my mouth. I don't know what to say to her anymore."

"She should be happy that you're alive."

"Oh yes that she is. People won't leave them in peace you see. Police come around and Miah's men too, to ask about my whereabouts. They tell them that they don't know. Baba got badly beaten. They tied up maa."

"All this must be really hard to talk about. But thank you for sharing. Is there anything else you want to say?"

"What else? No, none. Would no one take a shine to me ever? I don't want to be tinkering all my life doing nothing."

"You won't. Be strong now, so you can deal with life's difficulties later."

"Yeah. Thanks."

"Goodbye, Pontu. Come and talk to me anytime you want, okay?"

Pontu came out of her office feeling slightly upbeat. Life's paradoxes were strange. Hard work always didn't pay off. Who would intervene on his behalf? Man or God? It was almost like waiting for divine intervention to take place. Men had so much power over others. People with strong cases and weak were all in the same boat. All were running away from oppression of some sort. Evidence? Where was he going to get all this evidence from? In this culture, documents were taken seriously. But not in the Lost Winds. Nothing is well documented under the regime there. If any, they often look fraudulent here. He arrived hardly with any clothes at all; and certainly no passport. There was no evidence of an alleged crime. How did one prove ones innocence? Yet, he would die a terrible death in the hands of those who set him up. That indeed was the truth.

All the niceties of the world were a mirage to him. Fame, wealth, power, and happiness were lures revolving around him. Somehow, he was not a part of it. He felt he existed in a parallel world with only a 'see through' button. He could look, but could never be in it. Like the forbidden fruit, not permitted to enjoy, as though these impossibilities were hardwired into his system. Burn it. Oh! Burn it all. There was no need for art to flourish; no music to sooth the mind; no latent talent to be recognised. Barrenness was all that there ever was. However, he harboured strong passions to become someone; he waited for his ambition to flower, as the world prepared to impede it.

Pontu sat down to eat his lunch. He toyed with tomato skin in his food. Today, it was a meal from the Serendipa. Every dish came with the tinge of a sour and sweet taste. He picked at his yoghurt, and smiled remembering the young Confidante lady. He managed that conversation in broken Kroll language. Warmth grew in his heart for the lady. He was curious to find out if she was married. No matter; he discarded the unwarranted thoughts. When night fell over the mountains of the camp, he sat down in his room rummaging through all kinds of thoughts. That was mostly what he seemed to be doing these days, besides attending Kroll classes, training, gym and sports. He watched TV for a while and then prayed. Then he went to bed. Sleeping was one of the hardest things to do in camp. Not until quite late, would he actually get some sleep during intermittent night-mares.

Between those troubled hours of sleep and awakening, he heard maa's frantic screams; it echoed through his disturbed mind. 'Run boy run. They're coming for you.' Pontu ran breathlessly through the alley, by the Mohammadan house of God. His little chest heaved, tight with fear. Motor-bikies surrounded him; men in dark glasses in hot pursuit came to take him away.

"I don't want to, no, don't want to," Pontu cried in a child's thin voice. "I don't want to be a part of all this. I don't want to throw bombs at people, rocks, kill and plunder. In the name of resistance, God save me, I shall be growing up doing all this. Oh, I want to go to school, read and to write."

But they were resolute. They picked him up without hesitation, took him away and put him to work. It was recruitment; it was awful.

'Leave me, leave me alone,' Pontu screamed in bed. He woke up sweaty and frightened in the boot camp. Red streaks across a pale sky, told him that it was time for the early morning-prayer. Patience was a virtue. Did he have an option besides being patient? Yet, life came with no promises or guarantees. Fleeting moments or small indulgences leading to nothingness was the only guarantee. Mega dreams and aspirations were notional; they served a futile persuasion for recognition, only to be followed by grand deceptions, central to life's contradictions. Get better at your task. Push the limits and the boundaries; freedom and fame lay ahead. Happiness is but elusive for as long as it lasted like caffeine in a cup of coffee. A pat on the shoulder that one had done better than a few million others appeared to be all important, somehow. Pontu was ambitious. He wanted to give his life another chance; he wanted to reload every bit that he had missed out on; education and employment were just some to begin with. He called maa impulsively one day.

"Maa, I'm going to get out of here, I know."

"How long? Pontu, how long?"

"I don't know. But I've got to be patient, maa, pray for me. To be patient is all we ever do now," he said. "Is baba, better?"

"The wounds seem to be healing."

"Did any one come to investigate?"

"Yes, yesterday, some people did come. I think they were just the police from the local station."

"You need to send my school certificate maa. This will get me a job here in the end."

"Okay. Keep trying Pontu. Never give up."

"I'm trying maa. I'm doing everything they ask me to do; couldn't try any harder."

"Are you praying regularly?"

"Yes, I'm, but the man who got killed recently, also prayed regularly, maa."

There was silence on the other end. Pontu stooped low and sat down on the camp grounds; silence on the other end.

"Maa, you there?"

"Yes, Pontu, I am. He was just unlucky."

"Is it in our hands to change fate? What is luck?"

"Learn the ropes Pontu, bye."

"Bye maa."

Luck and fate were meaningful concepts to a rider in a world determined to establish free will; this world, the Draviland, where pre-determination was obsolete. Learn the ropes. Being talented or truthful no matter how legitimate, did not always guarantee success. Men died in the Red Sea. Some survived with tremendous luck, saved by dolphins, those stories were true too. Life's journey was at odds. It could pass without fully understanding exactly what we were supposed to do here; what paths to take and what the cosmic plan of our existence was. Riders were leaving the camp, every day. But Pontu's day of release never came. He suspected that perhaps more papers were required; evidence, more and more of them to fully satisfy the high counsellors of the Draviland of his innocence. Time would pass unimpeded just like the slow water down the drain;

invaluable. For each invisible minute lost, here was an irrevocable addition towards infinity. Life was too short.

Pontu was of average height for a man. He was dark and plump. He lacked sophistication, confidence and stammered when he spoke. A fine line of moustache was just beginning to emerge on his upper lip. Clothes given from the camp were his only possessions, besides a mobile, which he had bought from Mundip. Calling maa and having a conversation with her ever so often, made his day. One day he went to see the Confidante. He sat across the table from her one morning, as he spoke with her in his usual broken Kroll. She noted that he squinted often and looked at the floor continuously. Pontu was afraid to make eye contact today.

"Pontu, tell me why you wanted to see me today."

"I want to tell you something."

"Okay, what is it that you want to tell me?"

"My maa grieves for me every day."

"I'm sorry to hear that your mother is so heart-broken."

"How can I prove that I had nothing to do with that murder?"

"Provide papers."

"What evidence? I'm innocent."

"Do you have a court case? Have you been charged with murder?"

"A case has been filed recently. Maa said that the police think I did it."

"Unsettling," she said. "Oh, look, don't worry about it. Tell your mother not to worry. As "long as you're in camp, no one can harm you."

"When will I be released?"

"I don't know."

"Aww."

"Sorry. Have you told the counsellors of the high court everything?"

"I had lied first. I told them I came here because I was poor. The *Transporters* from Mundip told me not to tell them the truth. Also, I was afraid. Not understanding the system properly, I thought I would get into trouble here. After all, I was implicated in a murder case back in the Lost Winds.

"Have you told them your true story in your subsequent interviews?"

"Yes. But I could not tell them the date of his murder. I was confused and I gave them different dates at different times. This journey was arduous. 15 days out on the sea, without food and water. I wasn't thinking straight."

"You were confused. I'm sure they'll understand. Just tell the high counsellors that there has been an error," she said calmly.

"I ran away from many places. I'm tired of running."

"Yes, understandably. Just be patient, Pontu."

"I learn Kroll and play sports and of course train regularly, but I still get anxious."

"We will be able to help you with that."

"My life has been such a lie," he said impatiently.

"Why is that?"

"I am only 17. I wanted to go to school, study. Just didn't work out."

"Take solace from the fact that none of it was your fault."

"I had the same dream last night. Trying to run, but can't, couldn't run away. My fate was sealed; born with broken luck."

"Now, you're trying to set it right, yeah? You're doing something to amend it."

"I can only try."

"Don't underestimate the power of your strength Pontu. Each of us is talented in our own ways. You just have to find out what is it that you do best and then do it."

"Yeah. I was always fond of singing. I often played the flute in the village when I took my baba lunch," Pontu spaced out slightly.

"What does he do?"

"Who? My baba? He has a farm. I wish none of this had happened."

"I'm sorry."

"Yeah, so am I."

She left it at that. And as soon as he came out, he met two other riders who told him their release was imminent and that both had converted to Jesuit. Whether or not these releases were related to any covert operation of proselytising in the boot camp was yet to be seen. Pontu had battled all along, but never thought of using religion as a means to an end. The banality of evil had caused him misfortune, but had never really made him entirely Machiavellian.

In the village, maa often fed Pontu out of love. Lunch was ready for baba, his father. Maa made up a plate full of rice, with some green papaya on the side and a raw onion. Pinch of salt, and green chillies were placed on one corner of the plate as well. She covered the plate with a lid and put two smaller bowls on top. One container carried a watery fish dish, the other bean soup. Then the pile of containers was tied up together in a red cotton kitchen towel, looking like the leaning tower of Pisa. He held a small pitcher of water in the other hand.

"Pontu dear, take this to baba."

"Okay maa," Pontu replied.

Pontu invariably left the task at hand to obey maa in carrying out her order. Maa's face would brighten up with a smile at his small shape leaving the house. Pontu walked for about 15 minutes down the dirt road in his tiny penguin gait to meet baba. The farmer had just finished tilling the land and was resting expectedly, waiting for lunch to arrive. He sat down under the shade of the Banyan tree and looked out towards endless tones of greenery. Pontu was nine at the time. His little body slowly appeared on the horizon, wearing a white shirt and black patched up shorts which maa had lovingly stitched up. Bare-footed the boy walked slowly leaning over the pebbles on the dirt road at times to avoid getting hurt. The farmer smiled at him, Pontu smiled back and put the several tiers down on the grass.

"Pontu, what has maa cooked today?"

"I don't know. Take a look."

He untied the red towel with his nimble, soft fingers and laid out a plate for baba. Then he sat cross-legged across him under the great Banyan tree and watched him eat; affection in his eyes simmered like a desert-mirage. After baba finished, he quickly packed the chaotic crockery in a bundle and then stood pulling himself up, smiling. He picked up the bundle and swung it over his shoulder before he turned around to step out. Setting off for home, on his way, he always stopped to pick up yellow mustard flowers from the side of the narrow dirt path for maa. Maa would have bathed by then and waited for him to come back and have lunch with her. Serving two plates of food, maa waited. And when he entered, she happily looked at him and invited him to sit by her.

"Come. Let's eat now. I want to feed you today, sweetheart."

"Okay maa."

That was such a treat, when maa warmed up to him like this, occasionally feeding him sticky fish balls fried in deep oil. He would run back to her, placing the towering stack under the running water tap. Poverty was always there. However, so was love and care in the big picture. Pontu's eyes glistened with love, feeling special and pampered; his face would glow through a child's downy, dark, skin under a mass of oily hair pasted to his scull like wet cow dung, glued on to the thatched walls for dry manure.

"Maa, I'll always stay with you when you grow old. Way much older."

"You would? You would have your own life by then with children and a wife and my little grandchildren."

Pontu rolled up his eyes in embarrassment.

"I'll take care of you maa, so you never have to work so hard. And I'll make sure that baba never has to work in other people's fields again. We will buy our own land. Become rich, work for ourselves."

"You're a good boy Pontu. Have you done your homework for school?"

"Yes, I have, teacher said I did well in language."

"Good boy, no sooner you will be helping baba in the fields."

"I'm afraid to go to the house of God."

"Why?"

"Men on a Honda tell me to go with them."

"Go with them? Where to?"

"They tell me and other kids to go to meetings and rallies. They tell us to hurl rocks at others."

"Oh my God! Stay away from these people."

"Yes, maa."

A long way away from home now, Pontu sat at the boot camp and heard echoes of his own sobs. Men succeeded in recruiting him and many others like him in the end.

One midsummer afternoon, as he was returning from the Mohammadan house of God, they caught him on the dirt road and took him off to the city. He had turned ten at the time.

"Let me go! I want to go home!" he had cried out.

"We would kill your baba and maa and then take your only sister away."

Pontu fell victim to that and could not utter another word. He had stopped going to school and he found himself running errands for the resistance party instead. He did what he was asked: brutally recruited children. Friends, he played with, so they too would distribute leaflets and brochures for the party. Jobs then escalated to a much higher and disappointingly to more heinous and dangerous crimes; torching cars; hurling rocks; beatings and brawls and arguments. On the streets of Potteiclay in the city, Pontu was seen one evening with blood-shot eyes, sprinting frantically through a violent mob with cocktail in his hand in tattered shirt, blood running down his left cheek; marks of beating stood out in red hot streaks criss-crossed on his back. Soullessly, it behooved him to keep up his end of the bargain, so his mother, his father and his sister would be protected. He escaped from one prison to the next. All in the name of democracy and freedom which in the end became an excuse to grab more power; patriotism was never a part of this zeal. However, ensued by a fall out with the party in the end, it betrayed him by making him a scapegoat in a murder case. Maa had been mute with fear and baba could not protest. It was too late, too late now to go back to that golden age of purity. Oh Pontu, how you have corrupted your soul?

Pontu walked up to the gym down the grassy path of the camp. With a few other riders, he waited for his turn on the treadmill. As soon as one got off, he quickly got on and did a run for half an hour at the speed of six. Then he went into the shower. Next was Kroll class. Here, very attentively, he concentrated on listening skills today. He had to master Kroll, if he were to get ahead, one of the ropes to success. He had to convince the authorities that he wanted to be a model citizen.

"Hello, how're you?" a voice in the tape asked. Pontu parroted first and then said, "I'm well, and you?"

Turquoise Roots

MD got off the bus. He waited for Angella to pick him up. She was not here yet. Strange, MD thought, he had expected to see her waiting for him, as soon as the bus arrived. West Mountains stood in the backdrop, with all its alluring blue haze; the clouds floated straight into its summits. Craggy and green, the stalwart peaks stood the ravages of time. A smile emerged on his thin lips. He knew he was in love. In the village there was a massive banyan tree whose age old roots stretched over, under and through the brown earth in tortuous hamper. Pael was almost falling over; he moved swiftly to grab her and then held her in sweet embrace. Pael had giggled and jumped up to reach the nearest branch on the tree for a swing.

"I hope, I don't ever have to move from here."

"We'll go abroad, Pael, I'll take you abroad. I saw in movies, there're a great many nice places around the world that we can see, much better trees than these; although, I like this one too."

"Yeah? And where would you go? Do you have money?"

"I'll make money."

Pael had laughed her head off. He had not paid any attention to her taunts. For he knew a day would come when he would step outside this perimeter. Now, he smiled at the thoughts that he was actually travelling; he was in the West Mountains. It was not just the roots of the banyan tree that were twisted, so were

116

his own emotions, oscillating in the dilemma of his pledge and his new found existence in the West Mountains. Fulfilling those promises appeared to be remote.

There she was. Angella was here. Her Toyota sedan swung around and parked alongside the bus stop. She waved at him and opened the door for him to step in. He stooped forward to pick up his bag and entered the car.

"Sorry, for being late," Angella apologised, turning a smile on him.

"Okay, okay," MD smiled back.

Angella put the car into drive and slowly eased out of the spot.

"So, do you like it so far?"

"I like, very beautiful, mountain, I like."

"Yeah, they're beautiful, aren't they?"

MD nodded in agreement.

"Tell me, how was the ride?"

"Good. I sleep."

"Oh, that's good. At least you can sleep on a trip, unlike some."

MD didn't reply. They drove in silence for a while, taking in the pleasure of this serenity. There were just a few cars on the road. By far the smallest amount of traffic he had seen since his release from the camp.

"It's a bit quiet out here. But you'll get used to it after awhile."

117

"No. Good. I like."

"Oh good, then you won't be too bored, I hope."

"No. No. Village quiet like this,"

"What's your village like? Tell me."

"No good, no peace."

"Well, you're here now. Safe."

MD kept quiet. He thought of his permit process and the mugger at the park. Angella felt she might have touched a nerve.

"No matter, we're going to have a bbq party tonight. I meant to have it for a while now. What better time than this?"

MD smiled. He was pleased and felt warmth in her heart from her welcome. Being judged, vilified and demonised were the experiences of most of the riders that came by *Blue Moon*. They came here to take this land away was the general feeling, not to mention jobs. People had not actually stopped to think of the unaccountable number of jobs created on account of them and money made as a result. Charity organisations never saw the days of kaput, since their arrival. Economic reasons or not, if people died from starvation, in any part of the world, they had the right to move. And they did so, through whatever avenue was left open for them. That was human instinct. Human history was made of natural migration. Like migratory birds, humans had always moved from one place to the other; something they must do both here as well as on earth with one moon; if they had not left the Urals, then Magyars would not have made their presence felt today in one of the most historic places of the world, Hungary. Time would stand witness to this kind of human exodus. The modern era was, ironically, less sympathetic to this for all its worldly wisdom and chronicles in the archives.

The fact was, history always recorded such migrations indiscriminately. Today, it was the riders from the Southern Kingdoms in the planet with two moons. Past observed European colonization of the Americas on earth, Moors' of Andalusia, Spanish colonization over the Mayan civilisation in Mexico, and British over the aboriginals in Australia. Colonization was a kind of migration too. Only they were done by a superior class of people. Land was lost to victors and so were lives, but history continued relentlessly. Those who survived these ravages of time lived yet another day to tell the tale to the future generations. For better or worse, these acts were unstoppable. By far riders never intended to colonise. Rights were denied to people with impunity. Be it in Draviland or in the Lost Winds. Poverty could make them eligible. As member of special class, they could be accepted as a rider. But authorities recklessly ignored that. Thousands may die from poverty all over the planet, but when such people were assessed, they were not successful. Folly and ignorance on the part of the assessors might have been the root cause for not understanding their issues perhaps, but their unfettered cries remained forever suppressed. Riders were often persecuted for freedom of speech in Lost Winds, which qualified them to become riders, but getting amnesty in Draviland was nowhere close either. Whether it be for political reasons or economic, the boot camp ultimately became a metaphor of perpetual anguish, true to their own circumstances in life.

The car eventually drove over the driveway to Angella's house. It was a nice house with tiles on the roof and a brick facade, which was a reminder of the last one that MD had shared with his friends. Ties with them were like deep roots of the Banyan tree existing within his soul. Nonetheless, new ones had to be made, if one were to embark upon this life. New friends were needed.

"All good?" said Angella smiling."Tomorrow we go to the Sunday markets. How does that sound?"

He liked the sound of that. Sunday market. He had never been to one before. MD opened the door quietly and let himself out of the car. His only luggage was his back pack, which he was already carrying. With Angella leading, MD inhaled a deep breath. Air surely felt fresh in the West Mountains. Freedom was not an option anymore; it had to be achieved at any cost.

Angella opened the front door and they entered through it, one behind the other. It was a neat living room with a grey coloured old style sofa and an ottoman, with three other bedrooms in the house, MD had the one in the western corner of the villa from where, he would discover that the sun could be seen setting every evening. It was late afternoon and Angella put the kettle on as she showed him around. MD was free to use the kitchen as he pleased, cook whatever he wanted to, for both or for himself. No one would pressure him into doing anything he didn't want. That was the impression Angella was giving him. She lived in this big house alone. If she had a family that was hard to decipher from the pictures she had showcased on the mantel piece, which were all with her pets, cats mostly. She grew up on a farm. Animals were all she ever loved, besides her parents and siblings. Those who lived around her were mostly her three brothers, who owned farms of their own. Teacher@retired, Angella worked as an educationist teaching history in state schools around Draviland for about all her life. She never married, but raised a child she had adopted from Jenoa of the east, years ago; a girl who would be about MD's age today.

MD left his bag in his room and sat down on his soft bed. It was a small but cosy room; with just a few basic furniture such as a desk with a chair and a single bed with one bedside table. He heard Angella pottering in the kitchen and immediately came out to give her a hand. He brought some cups and saucers out of the cupboard and a plate to put biscuits on, when he saw her taking arnotts' out of its wrapper. Angella set a table for two and poured tea.

"We've had this tradition of tea for many years in our family," she said.

"Tea, what meaning? Please"

"It means dinner to some people. We don't call it dinner, but tea. I am going to serve minced meat soup with a bowl of salad tonight. And blueberry muffins for dessert."

"Food, same every day?"

Angella laughed.

"No MD, it doesn't have to be same every day. You can surprise me with your cooking skills sometimes."

MD smiled and sat down to eat tea with Angella at the kitchen table. It was a neat little kitchen, with a stove and a counter top and built-in cupboards, a fridge, and a dishwasher. Red and white stripe kitchen towels hung from an overhead hook on the wall. It was the beginning of an end which had started now.

"So what do you think so far?" Angella asked, digging her fork into the salad bowl."

"Good, good, my room like."

"I like my room," Angella corrected.

"Thank you. I learn more here."

"Yes, much more than you would normally from class," she said, staring blankly. "I once had a home stay student from Jenoa. He learnt quite a bit of Kroll language before he went home."

"He go back?"

"Yes, he was a student who stayed here for three months, in your room," Angella replied.

MD looked down at his food and finished the rest of it quietly. He enjoyed the soup and the salad. Tea was over. He picked up the dishes and cleared the table. Angella stood abreast with MD and helped him with the wash and the wipe. She noticed how diligently MD soaped each dish and cutlery. Instead of soaking those in suds filled basin water, he picked each up individually and poured a drop of soap in and wrung the sponge around the dishes. Then he rinsed them until they *squicked*. Angella watched the devotion he put into his work. She was more than happy to have him around.

"Angella, how say off and out?'

"Oh you take something *out* of fridge and take the magnet *off* the fridge, like this," said Angella stripping a magnet off the surface of the fridge and taking a bottle out of it. "Off versus out. That's how it works in the Kroll language."

MD learnt immediately. He was a fast learner and Angella, a good teacher. Later that night, he sat down at his desk when she went to bed. She said she felt tired. He decided to write a letter to Nalia. In his first language, he wrote.

Dearest sister,

I think I'm going to settle in very well here. I know everybody is angry with me for embracing Jesuit religion, but this religion is not all that different from Mohammadan you know. The concepts of hell, heaven, purgatory, charity are in fact very similar concepts, I've come to learn. What I've learned more, however, is of universal love. How love, care and nurture can transform life. Pastor Patrick and now Angella, my two new friends and land lady here have given me so much support that it is beyond description. I can never pay back their debt. They cried when they heard my story. They cried even more when they heard how dolphins saved me at sea. I'm sure you might have heard about the dolphins by now. These are stories from the heart, Nalia, from the diary of a rider. I told them that as soon as the sea unworthy vessel began to break, I was terrified. Barely, somehow, I hung onto a raft floating by. Nothing, but water all around, in the middle of this menacing ocean, survival was impossible. I started praying, crying in horror with my feet dancing under water. And then there were these dolphins that appeared from nowhere; they totally surrounded me. I couldn't tell you how they arrived, but they were there. I felt they were urging me to swim with them and I started to swim without thinking. And then a fishing boat came by. These sea-farers took us on board until our boat was intercepted by the Dravi guards.No news from the high counsellors yet. I continue to be in touch with them with my updates. I feel like a foot ball player. The closer I push the ball towards the goal post, the harder it becomes. But I am hopeful that one day I shall push the ball hard and strategically enough for it to go in. I shall have pocketed the game then. Tell Pael not to wait for me. I don't know yet when we can be together. Youth passes like slow slither of sand through the fingers; the very essence of life. I love her dearly; I always have and always will. I wish I could have her by my side now, more so in the West Mountains, nothing short of a paradise. I feel my love for Pael gets stronger, as it meets here at the focal point of the two angles; my love of the West Mountains and my love for her. Sacrifices need to be made unfortunately. That is reality in short.

The authorities are averse to the riders' cause. They're in a bit of a crisis themselves, I think. The name of the high counsellor is Patrick Wembly. They can't seem to be passing a single policy through the court. There have had a lot of issues with permits of residence lately debating whether or not riders should be granted a permanent or a short term one. Our fate hangs in the balance. I don't know what will happen in the end. Nobody knows it seems, not even the givers of permit. But it behooves not just me, but anyone in my circumstance to be kind to people, as they have been to me. Generally, I have been infinitely lucky with the Dravi, as I have been with father and mother and those who helped me come this far; ironically, not quite so with my biological parents. One of those random paradoxes, I believe. No matter, give my regards to father and mother and tell them that I pray for them every night before I go to bed. I shall inform them as soon as a break through comes along. Not long now, being an orphan and a Hingyan, come to think of it, I never was a citizen of any country. Was I? Now this might actually work in my favour.

Love you,

Your dearest brother,

MD.

P.S. Please say hello to Pael for me and ask her where Pontu is. I shall try very hard to keep my promises to her.

MD left the letter inside his writing book that he used for Kroll classes. Then turned off the lights and went to lie in bed. If there was one thing about him that set him slightly apart from everyone else in his situation was this optimism, not necessarily his naivety.

Next day, MD woke up early. He went out in the garden under the streaming golden sunlight. He found out that work was needed to be done around the house. Lawns were unkempt. There were a few broken tiles on the roofs; the gutter on the roof needed to be cleaned, so on and so forth. He decided to put himself to work as soon as possible. If Angella was going to teach him Kroll, the least he could do to pay her back was by making himself useful around the house. Today, was market day. They were going to buy barbecue meat, bread and salad for the party. MD made himself, a cup of tea and waited for Angella to wake up. He needed tools to fix this place up. He took a sip standing out on the lawn.

Soon Angella came outside to join MD. They greeted each other cheerfully and set off for the market through the fence gate. It was a mere half an hour walk. Music akin to *'row, row, row the boat gently down the stream, merrily, merrily, merrily, merrily, life is but a dream,'* wafting through the air, as they walked closer. They sauntered through the market as companions that autumnal morning, looking at great many stalls, food, patched quilts and wood work. Buying things and consulting with each other, the market had its way of slowing people down as they made their decisions over ripe fruits, vegetables, fish, taut tomatoes and red hot chilli peppers. MD picked up some, so did Angella, paying separately for the produce. A friend said hello to

Angella, raising a hand and waving towards her. She and MD stopped to say hello too.

"This is MD, my new tenant."

"Hi, MD did you say?"

"MD."

"Oh MD, well I'm Steve, I own a sheep farm up north."

"Hi," said MD, flashing a guileless smile of white even teeth.

"Been up to a sheep farm ever? "

"MD is learning Kroll. But no, I don't think so."Angella jumped in.

"You heard what's happened in Badgerys Stream, I hope.

"Yes, terrible,"

"Can't be' too careful these days."

"So true. We'd better run along then."

"Take care."

Angella waived and MD did exactly the same with a grin. Steve eschewed MD and waved back to Angella. Shopping was nearly finished. The musicians were packing up too. They slowly walked back home. One was a dark, stalwart young man, the other a sturdy middle-aged woman.

MD's letter finally reached the village. But no one opened it. Winds glibly carried it away in casual chase and whispers of ghastly horror through the bamboo bush. The house of the

Monsoon rain and the pretty pink knitting was now deserted; front yard had fallen decrepit as though struck with the dark fever of pestilence. Branches from storm lay randomly across the yard as did poles and the shack roof. Doors hung from their hinges, in the process of coming completely apart. Ravens came and sat fruitlessly in the yard in search of salted fish.

Emerald Luminosities

Murmuring softly, Murma flowed unhindered in an age defying spirit. Spring was in the air that year, touching the village blissfully. Migratory birds flew in from faraway places; Sparrows, Kingfishers, Red Beak Parrots and Cuckoos. Flowers bloomed at nature's beck and call; White Roses; Gardenias; Tiger Lilies; Golden Poppies and Lotuses in village ponds. Budding Rose petals opened wide and deep to catch a droplet of the morning's first dew. Indifferent to anyone's admiration, they wilted hastily away. Pael stood quietly under the Banyan tree; her sunken cheeks and long, windswept black hair marked the impression of a forlorn spirit. With undiluted expectations in her eyes, she gazed out at the river Murma, a witness to many broken promises and dramas.

Pael, Nalia, Tahu were playing here as children. They made swings with rope, tied it over the nearest branch. Nalia fell down and skinned her knees; Tahu's turn; Tahu swung herself to all time high up in the air; flew on it like a Sparrow; wind on her face; Nalia stopped for a breath; it was Pael's turn. Multicoloured pink frocks bright in the afternoon sun, Pael pushed Tahu all the way up and left her there to swing straight back. Nalia gave her a second push and Pael got her act together to give her a third with her small fingers, her lanky legs ran up and down the seat of the swing. Laughing until she coughed and singing like a lark, freedom and happiness were at the best of times. Tahu jumped off the swing and stood closeby waiting to push Pael back up on the swing. Boys came around shortly, MD, Pontu and Romeo, all in white, tight, praying caps and long praying shirts from the Mohammandan house of God. They joined in the merriment until dusk fell on the Murma in faded crimson.

Lost Winds appeared to be ghastly empty at present; silence; with just vultures scouring the sky, snooping for open carcass. A man, who called himself none other than the gravedigger, opened a grave and brought out a skull in the twilight; one that belonged to the wealthy farmer. He had died a few months ago. The futility of it all, thought the gravedigger, as he considered the skull. It was not wisdom but frailty that prevailed in the end. A moment's rashness led the path of this man's glory but to the grave. Pontu's maa and baba also met with the same fate; all perished not just with age alone, but with burdens of colossal sadness. Gravedigger rested under the Banyan tree. Earth soaked up death and decay like sponge to water in Lost Winds.

Each house in the village had suffered in the hands of these resistance recruits leading to mass exodus from the village. Boys became riders of a lost cause. It was but a war of a different kind. Persecution and torture came to be known as a way of life here. The village became a desolate wasteland. Not one day went by, when people weren't hacked to death. Presently, there would be no one left to die, no one left to be recruited. The pendulum would swing the other way.

By the river Murma there was a small tea stall where people gathered to talk politics of the day while they drank tea. Members of both the resistance and the autocratic regime appeared here one winter morning. They ordered tea and sat down on the two benches set in front of the tea stall. Built on stilts of bamboo poles, the tea boy crouched on a higher plain inside his shack of a shop and carried out business through a small vent. Tea was only a small part of it. Rice, wheat, cooking oil, salt and other needs were also sold here. An argument broke out among customers.

"Eh, your brother eloped with my sister."

"Yeah, what else was there to do?"

"Not marrying her would have been the obvious choice. But he didn't. That showed how little respect he had for our position in society. And my father had to pay dearly with his life."

"Did you expect my brother to leave *Resistance* and join yours?"

"That would have been prudent."

"How so? You're a bunch of autocratic power grabbing thugs, murderers and cheats. That's how you got your wealth and position."

"Yeah? Tell your brother to divorce our sister. Your family has neither money nor any social status. And in the wrong party too."

"What would you do if he didn't?"

"We'll go after him and beat the hell out of him."

"How dare you?"

A horrendous fight broke out at that. Rocks were hurled and stones were thrown at each other along with whatever else they found near them. The wooden benches, where they sat not too long ago, were now shattered to pieces. Eventually guns came out and shots were fired. In a flash, this became a battle ground of blood, rampage, and killing; heads were hacked and people's inert bodies lay amuck in the dirt.

The tea boy was frightened beyond words. It was not enough that all these days they came along and didn't pay for the tea they had. Nor did they stop wrenching money, ever so often out of this poor boy, trying to run a tea shop. Overnight, they turned this into a burial ground of the most heinous crimes. What was left of this enchanting village was nothing more than a place of complete chaos, where crimes prevailed over justice and hatred over love. Gradually, people tried to flee or stayed more and more away from home. Business or employment, nothing seemed to operate smoothly any longer. Nalia's family was one of the lucky few who could escape this onslaught. Those who had not or were unable to move, faced either humiliation, dispossession or death. Such was the state of the village. Whoever heard about war without a cause? Suffering without reason? But it happened. Disruptions happened for no apparent reasons. Tahu sat by the river Murma in a confused state of mind. She spoke to her dead son. Uncombed hair in dreadlocks, she had no clothes on anymore. Buck-naked, a boatman from a passing boat threw an empty sack at her to cover herself with. She bothered not to use it. It fell off her and lay on the dirt.

Mosquitoes Too many of them Swat them Mosquitoes Son did you eat and drink okay Guavas were gone I could not bring Guavas anymore I should be able to bring some rice I would cook some tomorrow Anyone bothering you Let me know I would knock the day lights out of them Life was but a dream Oh I just had a peek Saw afterlife Heavens purgatory I saw God just then Oh no no hungry cold Dont don not touch me you bastard I would kill you like I killed them Did you want me by your side Son Not long now Life was a dream This was reality What I saw just now was clearly real I saw I saw Did you want to know What

I saw Spirit dance Colours One two three four Those mosquitoes were horrible Why was life important It passed See how it went in a flash Finished Touch life No you could not touch life Feel life no could not feel life either Spirit was all Spirit was what I saw Nothingness Grand nothingness Deception

Tahu tried to hold something. Her hands went straight through the air as she stretched them out. Fingers parted and closed. She sat mumbling talking to her son, as she had a visitation from her little Casper, the friendly ghost. Society had abandoned her, condoned her, but she lived. While the lives of others were at peril, Tahu's was not. Not any more at least since her husband perished; of late, she did not even suffer a scratch. She thought life was an illusion. She had become invisible, and an outcast to the rest of the village.

Nalia Who was Nalia Look Nalia chased the dragonfly Fire in hell dreams Life was a dream Hell and heaven were dreams Gravedigger knew better People died Oh the sweet smell of death Flesh oh this mighty flesh where did it all go Where World of spirit earth water air fire Dreams Huge dreams Woke up one day Dreams gone Woke up to what Bones Sculls Gravedigger knew better Son my son Come to me Smile.

Tahu smiled an awful lot. In her reverie, she seemed to see things beyond, heard voices that commanded her to carry out orders. One such voice asked her to kill the rich farmer. It was a long wait. Longest that there ever was, but she did it in the end. Pael nearly spent a life time for MD to come back and to take her abroad. Great Banyan tree protected her under its sturdy branches and robust roof of leaves. Indignation filled her up thinking that MD might have made empty promises. However, she never stopped hoping. A boat would stop on the silvery waves over Murma one day and a tall young man would get off and ask for her hand in marriage. Except that ravages of time would not have left anything the way he appeared in her mind. 15 years had now passed and MD had aged.

Pontu had aged too for that matter. He had stopped calling since maa and baba passed away. Callously, death struck them one after another, as each died soon close to one and another. Call it natural death. One had a heart condition and maa died of grief. She died because she couldn't endure Pontu's suffering any more. That was all too simple a solution for Pontu's family. But Pael remained. She grew gradually older with every passing season, but she somehow wished that neither MD nor Pontu would look any differently.

A life time had passed and Pontu hadn't returned to the village. He was now 27. No one knew his whereabouts either. Pontu liked eating the soft fatty part on the silvery blade fish. Blade, in fact was his favourite fish. Growing up, they fought for the best piece of the fish, the head while their maa and baba sat smiling at them. They wished that the fish had more than just one head. Maa had then decided to cut it in half so they would each have a portion at least. After Pontu left, Pael could have had all the head that she wanted, but she never touched it again.

Once being recruited, Pontu went to live in the city, and had to live a few days in the home of a rich leader there in Grosnii. They fed him sometimes, other times didn't; certainly never the head of a blade fish. Later that year when he came back to the village, maa had asked him intensely.

"Did they not feed you?"

"No, not much."

"Were you hungry a lot?"

"A lot, a lot of the times, I thought about you too."

Maa went silent after that.

Nalia in the city remained just the same as Pael was in the village. Nalia decided not to marry again. Milking those cows in the big house of her employer and then doing the chores in the house took a lot out of her. Mother helped when she could, but she was getting old by the day. Nalia had no knowledge that MD had written to her 15 years back, for she was 25 now. She was looking for it. Where was the milk jar now? Nalia panicked. There was no reason to panic but she still did it. Fretfully she went about the house looking for it. She poured herself a glass of water and drank it so fast that half the water fell out of her mouth, over the thin rim of the glass. She left half the floor undone, dirt lay everywhere around, as she quickly got up to do the laundry. Unfinished, she moved to the next chore, cooking. Anxiety gripped her so much that she wanted to finish everything all at once and wanted to resolve all her issues this very minute. Impatience; and that would be the correct word to use to describe her present mental state. 'Oh Tahu if only you knew, how it hurt to be away from the village. This drudgery would kill me one day. Since the death of their girl, my employers have left everything to me. They ate, if I prodded them. They wouldn't go to bed, if I didn't take them'. 'Tahu, father drove mother crazy sometimes over cow's milk, when he took it to people's homes to sell it. Mother would be forced to go with him. She needed to be with him at all times. At times mother felt suffocated. No respite. I often wondered at night, as I lay sleepless in my cold bed, how MD was? We wouldn't be in his memory anymore and that hurt. Today, I found some time to do knitting. I sat here in front of the gorgeous setting sun, when the clouds were dissolving into pink. My pink sweater is nearly there, my story is finished knitting. Nalia thought of returning to the village many times. Her eyes lightened up at the thought. Pael wrote her a letter saying that the village might be a safer place now, since the death of the farmer and those two ruffians who had made a threat to Nalia's father. Nalia and her family could try and return to the village if they pleased. Economic line was more or less set in the city and the people who employed her depended heavily on her and would not wish to see her leave, but she missed the village. She missed the trees, and the river. Silvery Murma accentuated into a deeper shade, when clouds gathered in the distant sky in an assembly of grey; winds picked up and blustered over the river. Hoary winged pigeons flocked together high up in the sky. As they turned their course of direction, they flew amazingly in an orchestrated synchronized dance. Nalia spoke to her parents one evening.

"Why don't we return home?"

"Where?"

"Village."

"What's left for us there?"

"The farmer has been ruthlessly murdered."

"Who told you that? Who could take him out that easily?"

"Someone obviously did. Nobody is interested in our house anymore. It's abandoned property."

"Really?" said Nalia's mother. "Let's just take our cows and go then? But our house..."

"What about it?"

"Can we move in just like that? I hope the regime has not confiscated it by now."

"No. Not yet. We should move in straightaway. Clean it up, cook salted fish in the front yard. You can make us sugary cups of tea, while I continue to knit until this story has ended."

"Is this a dream?"

"No, it's not. It's where life will begin anew. It's where rice will grow again. Earth will come around to full rotation."

"That's a wonderful idea."

"Yes it is. That's what we would have to do. Let's just do it."

Home was where the village was. Shingdi was poetry located only in the mind. Village was reality. Everything ever imaginable was possible in Shingdi. But the village was not such a place. Nalia and her family were yet to decide. Pael, Tahu were also there to welcome them back, although Tahu lost her mind quite beyond repair and recognition. Half eaten guavas would be left by her side sometimes, in the hope that she would be saving them for babu.

Burn in hell Burn People bad people burn in eternal damnation Heaven there was no heaven Sin guilt all in this world Bird came and bird went out of its cage Spirit of the body God Punishment surely My nails black and blue hands bruised Of Blood look at

blood Red spillage on the bed White sheets pillow Man dead
mangled body Pills bandage sanitised smell of Dettol
everywhere Doctors in white Nurses pushing stretchers into
operation theatre Hospital bed wealthy farmer was well and
truly dead MD safe Nails broken and bruised and blood clot
Blackened... Then she stopped whispering and flashed an
empty look. She would smile showing all of her teeth; those,
which were white once, now yellowing and verging upon red.

What if Shingdi did exist outside of the mind? Each could have
had the life that they wanted. Pontu could grow old here caring
for his maa and MD could marry Pael and continue to live in the
village. He might have owned a farm by now. Nalia could've
lived with her handsome Romeo in eternal bliss with children,
wearing her red untarnished bangles and red untorn clothes.
Sweet tunes from shepherd's flutes would be heard floating
through air all day long and each tree in the orchard would be
laden with ripened fruits. Half eaten fruits would be littered
everywhere by birds; fields packed with harvest. This would be
life where children would go to school happily. Their laughter
would ring in the air. Tahu would be raising her babu with love
and affection. It would be a place where people didn't sin. No
guilt would ever touch, certainly no terror. Their children would
be safe at school. No bullets, mortars or machetes would ever

burden life any more. But Shingdi was only a utopia, a figment of imagination that existed in pure poetry.

Sapphire Skies

MD sat down on the edge of his bed after dinner. He took out his diary and began to write. He dated it first and then wrote. There was still no news from the high counsellor's office. Backlog, they said jammed the flow. His belief was that perhaps the government wouldn't allow riders to stay here after all. Earlier on when he was cooking and watching television with Angella, he was dismayed to see how much aversion there was. One woman was interviewed who said that there was no need to debate in the high court about riders. Just turn the boats around! Why did we even need to talk about it? There was no room for riders on Dravi soil. MD looked at television and his jaw dropped to his chest. For all his optimism he could not but feel bleak about his future. Angella looked up at him and gave him a pat on his shoulder.

"Don't you worry MD, in your interview with the tribunal they might ask you about the Book and baptism. Show them how knowledgeable you are about the religion. Convince them that you're a practising Jesuit."

"I am."

"I know that but they don't."

"I know. They not believe. I not becoming Jesuit to stay."

"That's why I say, tell them that you've converted, because you wanted to, not to strengthen your case with the high court, okay? Odd that there would be so much conflict among us, the people of the Book, when there was none among the prophets."

"There was friendship between all the prophets of the Book. Why fighting we? All the time fighting."

"Spiritualism and religious politics are different issues MD." Angella responded somewhat delightfully as she considered MD's innocent disposition. MD smiled at that and lowered his gaze. He thought of the innumerable riders, with genuine reasons who were sent back to Lion's den simply because the high counsellors didn't believe their tales. They thought riders were not truthful; lying to secure permanent residency in Draviland. Some of them failed because they couldn't prove their cases with sufficient evidence. It was hard to know who lied though. Was it the counsellors or the riders? He was never able to get to the bottom of the problem. About 99% had to leave. Again some of these riders didn't leave inspite of the ultimatum, but kept buying time through various court appeals.

MD cooked eggs. Angella watched him boil them first as he placed four eggs gently in the water of a half filled up saucepan. 'These must be boiled well', he thought aloud. She watched him taking some onions and carrots and tomatoes out of the fridge and put them in a plastic bowl from the dish rack on the countertop. The idle cutting board was sitting on the countertop by the wash basin. He pulled a knife out of the knife rack from beside the stove and cut the two ends of the onion first. Then he scrunched off the layers of the brown dry skin. Angella picked up some of those skins off the floor and chucked them in the trash.

She walked up to the study and stood in front of her book case. Picking a poetry book, she sat down on an easy chair. What she read, resonated Omar khayyam's,

"Awake for Morning in the Bowl of Night..."

The cooking was starting to impart an authentic aroma of mixed spices; coriander, cumin and hot chillies. It was going to hit the spot today on flavoured Sun down rice. Angella made a small salad with market fresh tomatoes, cucumber and horse radish.

"How come, you not married?" asked MD over dinner.

"Oh, it's a long story. Maybe, I'll tell you one day."

They ate dinner in silence. Afterwards, it was Angella's turn to do the dishes tonight. MD had disappeared into his room and Angella into her study. She stood before the mirror and MD's question struck a chord. Yes, she could have married Peter Whyte. She did love him at the time.

One winter afternoon the breeze had blown hastily through the market. She stood in front of her father's apple stall with a bowl of sliced apples. She looked up at a wisp of fallen leaves off the

Cedar Wattle. Faded into lemon hues, they swept through the gust incongruently. A strand of hair blew over her cheeks, as she bumped into Peter Whyte. Purely by accident, they smiled at each other. She was barely just 18.

Angella heard MD pottering again in the kitchen. She heard him open a can.

"My name is Angella."

"I'm Peter."

"This is my father's stall,"

"All apples?"

"Yes, they're really delicious. Want to try some?"

"Yeah sure, why not,"

Peter picked a couple of sliced apples from the bowl that she held out. Sweet touch of his finger on her thumb set off the first shivers of romance through her spine. Peter liked the sour sweet taste as much as her confused look in those pure blue eyes.

"How old are you, Angella?"

"18."

"I'm 25, and a medical student."

"I am studying to become a teacher."

"Say, do you have some time? Why don't we go n' sit down under that big tree there and listen to some music together."

"Just a second. I'll ask dad."

"Sure. I'll wait."

Peter watched as Angella disappeared somewhere in the back of the stall. He waited for her in the gusty wind under the trying leaves of the Wattle branches. Angella reappeared.

"Sorry, I can't stay away much longer,"

"I won't keep you much longer."

They walked together under the big tree on a huge tortuous trunk. The sweet melody of the singer's voice reached the very core of their hearts. He laid a hand on hers and that was love at first touch. The translucent blue sweater matched perfectly with the same in her eyes. She smiled at him and he smiled back. The song ended.

"I need to get back. Help dad pack up."

"I want to see you."

"I'll be here next Saturday. Same time."

"Okay, see you then."

Angella left Peter there at the tree trunk, as she brisked back to the stall excitedly. Her heart thumped and her pulse raced. She saw her dad packing up. Quickly, she made herself available to him. But she could not hide the flushes on her cheeks. That was the first time that she felt like that. Belatedly, she thought she could have given him her address. Next week was long way away. At dinner Angella wasn't hungry. She went to bed early and found herself thinking about Peter. How he walked, leisurely and relaxed. He smiled lazily when she gave him that confused look; his warm touch. She could not get his handsome face out of her mind; tall, slim, blonde. He wore a thin beard that suited him perfectly. His blue eyes twinkled when he smiled. Angella never liked beard in men, but she liked one on Peter.

Angella's father was a farmer here in the West Mountains. He ran an apple farm with his wife, Aida. Angella was born on this farm with all her siblings. The family hadn't moved ever since. Together with her siblings, they had a happy life. They were raised as Jesuits, although Aida herself was a Mohammadan from Mundip. But she never resented it. She left it to nature to take care of the course of the events. In her simplicity she believed that as long as the family was well fed, there was no reason to rant after one another because of religion. She went to the Jesuit house of God with them as they did to the Mohammandan house of God when they were growing up. Love prevailed over religion in this family and that was the beauty of it. Once Angella's father, Ned, had asked her when the children were still quite young.

"Doesn't it bother you that your children could become Jesuits?"

"What would bother me more, if they turned bad or went hungry."

"Why is that? It would bother most people."

"I don't know. I think growing up in Mundip taught me a few good things about life and religion; that all prophets were to be respected regardless."

And that was the end of the discussion. The family picked fruit together on the farm when they ripened on warm winter afternoons and Aida made delicious apple pies and sauces for them at dinnertime in the large family kitchen. Days went by and Angella grew into this beautiful young lady, without even realizing the passage of time. Nobody on the farm bothered her much, neither did Aida. They lived and they let live. That's how life was. Complexity was never a part of this picture; neither were unscrupulous dealings with one and another. Angella would hear horrendous stories about her friends' parents' splitting up. It saddened her to see how this divorce and the domestic violence affected their lives. But she prayed to God thanking him for her lovely home and meals.

One evening Aida was baking blueberry muffins in her kitchen. Angella entered rather anxiously. Aida looked up at her in surprise. She sat down on a kitchen chair and burst into tears. Not understanding what was going on, Aida came by and sat with her. Angella was only six at the time.

"Mitsy is missing, I can't find her anywhere. I think something took her. She was here just now."

"What do you mean by *something*? You saw her here awhile ago, is that what you're saying?"

"Yes, yes. Can't you see, she's just gone? Vanished like magic?"

"Maybe she went for a walk. She will be back. Cats do that sometimes. I'll buy you another, if she's lost."

"How can you even say that? Buy me a cat. Who can replace Mitsy? A hundred cats couldn't replace her. Can't you see that?"

"Of course, I can see that Mitsy was special and unique. But you've got to let go of things sometime. Look, it has been what five minutes that the cat's gone missing? I'm sure it will be back."

"I know, cats go wondering about sometimes and Mitsy has done it too in the past. But this is different. I feel it in my bones that something's wrong. Someone took her. I just know it."

"Don't jump into conclusions just yet. Wait a while. Maybe she's gone a bit longer than usual."

"I don't know. Oh, I don't know," Angella began to cry uncontrollably.

Angella was right. Mitsy did disappear after that day, but she never bothered to get another cat. Aida tried to persuade her into having any number of cats she wanted, but Angella's loyalty for Mitsy was so great and her grief so profound that she believed that she would be better off without a cat, as no other could replace Mitsy. Aida had a sensitive child and worried how Angella was going to fit into this world beset with despair and disappointments. Nevertheless, Angella's love for poetry and literature grew beyond the national boundary and she attempted to read inter-galactic writers in languages other than Kroll. *The Rubaiyat* by Omar Khayyam; Charlotte Bronte's *Jane Eyre* formed her character. In fact, *Jane Eyre* was her role model who inspired her to be a teacher which she eventually became.

Meeting Peter Whyte was an incidental disruption in her life. Love for her was like a deity; the kind that Rochester had for Jane Eyre. Romance meant much more to her than just sharing life with an adorable partner, but expectation of an idealistic love, found possibly only in novels and poetry. When she met Peter, she thought she'd finally found it; the most amazing, romantic love that she'd ever sought. She imagined herself in Jane Eyre's place, but without her sufferings. She wanted to meet Peter Whyte in pink. When the *next week* arrived eventually, Angella took out a pink chiffon blouse and blue jeans and a turtle neck pink sweater. While the family loaded the van for the market, she stayed in front of the dresser touching up on the mascara. Aida knew that her daughter acted differently, but tried not to interfere in her affairs. She gave her time to sort out her own life.

She appeared finally looking simply pretty. A classical nose set above her full pink lips. Curled lashes overhung with heavy thickness down that large opal-eyed loveliness. Fair, soft skin, milky white was as untarnished and smooth like a new-born's innocence. Her hair, shimmering, cascaded all the way to her slim waist.

"Ready to roll Angel?" Ned said.

"All good," replied Angella with a shy smile.

Angella was first to get out of the van. She helped them unload and unpack, but Aida told her not to worry today and smiled secretly at Ned. The stall was set up once again and Aida cut up slices of apples in a bowl and handed them to Angella. All morning passed, she did not see Peter. Today, she was going to give him her address. In the afternoon, she waited under the same tree with sliced up apples in the bowl and watched people saunter through the path. Some picked up a slice, while others simply bought apples straight from the farmer. They grew the best apples it appeared in all of West Mountains. Peter still didn't show up as promised. The day progressed into the evening. The farmers began to pack. Soon it was time to leave. Aida put a hand on her silky white shoulder and smiled slightly. Angella was stood up and she didn't know how to handle this disappointment. They went home and Ned kept an eye on her sad face through the rear view mirror. By the time they reached home, it had become a crisp evening. Angella got out of the van and went straight into her room and shut the door. She had not come out for dinner or sat by the fire in the living room with her family. Aida's oven-baked roast had not given her an appetite either. Now, here was a situation that only time could heal. Inflexible as steel, Peter had commented about her the next time they actually met in the market two weeks after. He had taken her by surprise again. Peter just walked up from nowhere and stood in front of Angella. He kept his steady gaze up at Angella hoping that her frosty blue eyes would melt. But they hadn't. Rather they got sterner.

"You stood me up. What do you expect?"

"Can you calm down a bit and let me explain?"

"If you think you can take advantage of me you're wrong."

"Ow, wow, who's saying anything about taking advantage? On the contrary, it is your innocence that draws me towards you."

"This is hardly the place to discuss this."

"I agree, why don't you come with me up front? Under the tree."

"Okay, we'll talk."

"We'll talk."

Peter put his two hands up to his chest and smiled gleefully. His eyes twinkled yet again that swept Angella off her feet. She put the apple bowl down on the table and came out of the stall. Aida and Ned both saw them leave on the chilly afternoon.

Peter Whyte and Angella walked down the path in the market. He took her hand and caressed it tenderly. She didn't pull it away. He looked at her and saw her smile. Angella thought of Jane and Rochester under the chestnut tree. She thought what Rochester told her under that tree just before the lightening. He had kissed her; held her in a tight embrace; had said that he loved her and treated her as an equal.

"Come let's sit here," said Peter pulling her towards him.

"Oh, I nearly tripped, Peter," said Angella laughing, as she just managed to avoid a twisty root causing her to fall.

"Which school did you go to Angella?" Peter asked.

"Warrinarri Public School. Why do you ask?"

"Just wanted to know. You're sheer poetry; haven't really met anyone quite like you."

Angella laughed flashing her white pearly teeth.

"Really? Unbelievable."

"Why unbelievable?"

"Better or for worse?"

"Interesting. Neither. Just no one like you."

"It was really, really nice meeting you too, Peter, although you did stand me up."

"Do you want to know why that happened?"

"No, not really. You're here, now that's all I need to know."

"Okay. So what do you plan to do next?"

"Well, I can write down my address to you, and my phone number."

"That would be nice. How about going to the movies with me sometimes?"

"I'll have to ask mum and dad."

"Sure, tomorrow evening?"

"Okay, pick me up at six."

Peter nodded, as he wrote her address down in the address book, with the phone number. They leaned against the trunk of the tree and watched a singer on the stage play a Dravi tune into her flute. The winter birds sat on a slender branch while a tranquil breeze passed by. They sat with their palms held together until they started to sweat.

"Time to go," said Angella quietly.

"Yes, I'll see you tomorrow."

Peter looked at her and gave a peck on each cheek. He smiled at the diffused pink blush on her face appearing almost spontaneously.

"Magical. You dropped a potion of your magic into me."

"I'm no enchantress. I'm just me." she smiled until her cheeks dimpled.

"Something about you. That look, those expressions..."

Angella smiled calmly and thought of Rochester caressing Jane Eyre in the library after the fall out. That he too had called her magician. She hoped she had the same effect on Peter; putting a spell on him too. Was she reliving Jane Eyre?

"I must go now."

"Okay, I'll see you soon."

Peter helped Angella get steadily up on her feet. He held the elbow of her left crux, as she bent backwards a bit before she straightened. She looked at him and blew a kiss and then left him there listening to the flute. Angella felt she soared like a lark today. Oh, what a feeling! She walked fast back to the stall, where her parents waited eagerly for her.

"Well, how did it go?" asked Aida with slight smile, cutting apples and eating slices.

"What do you mean?"

"You know?"

"Yeah, he's okay." Angella kept her cards close to her chest.

"Just okay? Or good okay?"

"Oh, I don't know. Let's go. I'm tired."

Ned had started to pack already. Angella went forward and gave him a hand with the boxes of apples that had to be loaded into the van. It would have been easier, if her brothers came along, but they had their own things to do on the weekends.

Peter Whyte was a class by himself. Cool; confident; knowledgeable. Although he was her first love, Angella had other admirers with whom she never ventured to go out. She might even consider marrying him if he proposed to her one day. In the evening before dinner, Angella sang an English tune, *"and I'll be there before the next teardrops fall"*, as she made salad with Aida. Aida opened the hot oven door and pushed the roasting pan in, then she turned around and closed it with a back-kick. Through the small oven window, potatoes, pumpkins and carrots glazed a golden colour set around the leg of lamb which she laboriously marinated last night. Ned was in the shed looking for a hammer to put up a picture of a kangaroo on one of the living room walls. Angella looked at Aida from the corner of her eye as she sliced up cucumbers to mix with the salad. Aida stood by the warm oven gazing at the golden vegetable and the leg of lamb sizzle gently on fire. The fire burned evenly passing on the warmth through the room. Ned entered with the hammer and began to hammer in a nail on the centre of the side wall. Once it was in place, he picked up the picture placed on the table and put it up, adjusting and readjusting, until he was satisfied that it was in dead centre.

Angella finished tossing the salad. She left it on the table and went into her room, while they waited for the lamb to be cooked. She closed the door behind her and took her sketch book out and the etching pencil. Sitting in front of her dresser, she began to draw Peter Whyte first and then turned the page to sketch a self portrait. Rightly or wrongly, the character Jane Eyre indeed captivated her quite completely.

MD was pottering as usual in the kitchen; opening cupboards, getting a glass out and drinking water. He didn't realise that Angella hadn't gone to bed. Angella was still in her study, day dreaming about her days which had passed incognito.

"Are you there MD?"

"Yes. I water drink. You alright Angella?"

MD asked inclining from his position in the kitchen towards Angella.

"Yeah, yeah I'm okay. Did you want to come into the study?"

"Sure."

MD put his glass down into the sink, walked towards the study and found Angella sitting in a reclining chair. Lifting a lazy hand, she signalled him to pull up a stool to sit down. Obediently, MD followed. Quietly, he watched Angella's face closely and decided that she looked slightly pale. Her unopened worn out diary and a sketch book were on the table. The frayed pages were evocative of the ancient castles of the Southern Kingdom.

"You wanted to know why I never got married."

"Yes."

"This diary will explain it and the sketch book."

She took the sketch book out and opened it to show MD the portraits of an unknown artist. In the romantic glow, Angella's wrinkles did not appear to be too prominent. If fact, she looked almost young. MD saw pictures of many young people and a cat.

"Who these are?"

"This is me at 18."

MD considered the picture and thought Angella was quite a beauty. And then the page turned to a young man.

"Who this man. Your husband?"

"No, MD. Not my husband, my lover."

"Why you not marry him then?"

Angella drifted off at the question as MD eagerly delved into the pictures.

Angella had just finished sketching. Aida got the roast out of the oven and called out Angella and Ned for dinner. They sat around the table and Ned took a spoon full of vegetables and potatoes while Aida cut a few slices of the roast meat off the bone. Angella ate very little. Ned looked at her quizzically and served her a bit of the same on the plate. Aida poured water in each glass. Angella started talking suddenly.

"I'm going out with Peter tomorrow night."

"Whereabouts?" asked Ned

"To the movies?"

"As in a date?"

"Yes, I think so."

"Now, you be careful missy."

"It's all right," Aida chimed in. "About time, the last thing I would want is to see my daughter ending up as a wall flower."

Ned ate quietly and so did Angella. Aida poured more water in her glass and took a few sips. She was thirsty tonight. Angella ate a bit and stood up to leave the table. Ned looked anxiously at Angella's quiet, serene face.

"She needs to learn quite a bit about life. Can't you see she's a bookworm?" Aida planted an idea.

"You might be right. She's a bit of a nerd, isn't she?"

Then they quietly finished dinner.

MD glanced at Angella's blank look gradually spacing out into oblivion.

"Do you know what hurt me the most about Peter?"

"Name his Peter? You hurt?"

"Yes, MD. We moved in together for a year after I met him and then one morning he disappeared."

"Oh?"

"Without so much as a word, he left me, just like that."

Angella remembered. She went to the movies and they sat in a corner in the dark; first a peck on the cheek and then a wet, passionate full on kiss on her lips. Angella still felt the tingling sensation down her body, the raised hair on her arms and back of the neck. She cried out.

"Oh Peter, that was just perfect. I think I'm in love with you," she said lowering her eyelids. Peter glanced at her intently almost trying to open those eyelids with his look.

"You think? C'mon girl let's go home. Let's not waste time here."

Peter was breathing heavily and fast. They didn't wait for the movie to finish. Peter drove them straight to his place. Angella waited silently in the car as her stomach anxiously knotted and unknotted with excitement within. It was a night of remembrance. Soft fire burned steadily in the hearth of Peter's one bed-room apartment. They lay together in bed. Angella's naivety amused him, as he gently stroked her, her lips and her forehead. Angella enjoyed just as much as he did. She found Rochester in him and acted Jane Eyre for him.

Unlike Rochester, Peter Whyte was diabolical. One could love the Byronic nature in Rochester but not what Peter Whyte stood for. Her lack of worldly knowledge blinded her so she couldn't see it coming. If anybody was over whelmed then it was her, not Jane Eyre As days went by, Peter and her relationship staled, until one day, Peter was no more. Angella couldn't find him anywhere around the house. Well and truly, he had disappeared just like her cat.

Angella extended an arm to fetch the diary. She leafed through the pages and read loudly. 'You could call me inflexible. And I guess I'm a bit. But of all the admirers I've ever had, Peter was the one I loved. When we sat together in the market listening to the music, I felt what he felt. We shared a passion, as melodies stole our souls momentarily away. A world of magic, it fell crushing down like a house of cards. That was my life. '
"You see MD, I couldn't see anyone else in his place. You understand that don't you? There could never be another," she heaved, "I had loved him. I was prepared to follow him to the end of the world. I'd be dammed if love wasn't blind. I lived too much into those books. I was a fool; I was charmed."
"No. Not fool. You like Pael. Only Pael for me. I no marry, no one if not her."
Angella listened carefully to what he had to say. It was midnight. Stars in the sky watched them as unspoken witness.

An eternity would pass unnoticed, but these two wouldn't change. MD's permanent permit finally arrived one day. His case had been assessed and he was recognised as a genuine rider, the orphan who was stateless. His linguistics skills improved as the Kroll syntax began to appear gradually.

Crimson Fields

"I can't believe it," Pontu said to a mate in Madura Island. He was completely ecstatic.

"Believe it," said his mate. "It's your day. Your day has arrived. You've arrived. All that miserable training has now paid off. You have passed all your tests and are now truly out of this boot camp, in other words. hell."

Finally, authorities did take notice. Accommodation, hotels, health and finances, everything was taken care of, except one; freedom. It became the forbidden fruit and a confusing word. No matter how much he may have wanted it, it eluded him like the fire flies of a quiet village night in the Lost Winds where he would catch a glimpse of them glowing intermittently in passing.

Fifteen years had passed since his release. He rented a shared house close to a Mohammadan house of God in Botany Bay. Not only that he prayed, but literally stayed in the house of God. His case still dangled without any permanent solution or even news. He became a mere statistics in the court books; authorities who stalled, buying more time, so Pontu could be removed once problems settled down back home in the village. He wasn't the only one. There were thousands of others like him. Some didn't have work permit, but lived on borrowed money from friends. Day in and out they lived in the hope that one day perhaps a permanent permit would arrive and they would be allowed to stay here.

Some riders hallucinated and committed suicide, because they couldn't take this any longer. Occurrences like these made hot television and radio news. In desperation, they would take their young lives in protest, as the courts took their own sweet time coming to a decision. However, they died not in vain because in the end they were the ones to make history. Uncertainty, hung thick around the aggrieved riders. When were they getting their permits? When were they getting rights to work? Their troubles were far from over, as the high counsellors harangued them ever so often that they would be sent back, if they couldn't convince the tribunals with their stories. Pontu, however, did not think he would commit suicide. Faith prevented him from taking his own life. It was not for him to make those choices, as the Mohammadan religion decreed, but God's. Each day, he hoped that good news would come and each day he was disappointed. This was a strange life. Unemployed, unmarried and unwanted, Pontu almost lost his mind in despair. It wasn't a prison. Not at least like the ones that he was acquainted with in Mundip, Madura Island or Grosnii, but of a different nature. It did not matter how many tribunals he went through, letters he wrote to the high counsellor; all of those proved negative. Like the *Old man and the Sea,* it appeared he too was put to the test; one of patience with rewards awaiting at the end to be snatched away ruthlessly. This was like another boot camp with new sets of rules.

In the eyes of law in the homeland, he was deemed as a criminal. Charges were laid and he must face court case to gain acquittal. Most likely it would find him guilty as he was up against people with high political connections. Justice hardly prevailed in a corrupt place. He believed that as soon as he landed, even after all these years, his chest would be shredded with black pointed bullets. Those enemies were still at large. Therefore, he resorted to praying. Once again, no one could come to his aide except God. Such deep was the conspiracy that it was hard to know who framed him; the resistance party or the autocratic opposition? Pontu screamed in his sleep and woke up shivering each night, sweaty and cold for he saw people attacking him from all sides pinning him down to the ground and striking him hard with the blunt dagger butt; 'run Pontu run,' maa squealed in the background.

Pink Honeycombs

When the natives returned to the village, the season had come
to a full circle. Mists and dew drops took the harshness out of
the daylight. Winter had just stepped in. The village was the
same, yet not quite so. Tahu sat by the river Murma with her
ponderings. Pael, awaiting MD's return, dreamed that he would
take her away from this drudgery one day. Nalia's father's
thatched house was a shambles of cobwebs and twigs. The roof
had broken on one end, as had the supporting poles of the small
veranda. Branches from nearly all the trees piled up in a derelict
heap out in the front yard. 'Lots of work needed to be done
here', thought Nalia's father. 'Well, at least those trouble
makers were gone.'

Nalia took her knitting out. She had bought more wool recently.
Looking around at this disorder, she began knitting. Her pink
sweater nearly touched the ground by now.
Slowly, a new life was going to be engraved out of this mess.
Like the phoenix, life rose again from the ashes of destruction.
Cows' went back to their shack with a calf which had joined
them about three months now. A bigger place was needed for
hay to be stacked up against the wall. Typically a green
vegetable patch around the yard was what this place had
missed in a year of frightful neglect. Nothing was right. Nalia's

mother sat down in the yard of the house, as did her father. Nalia looked around a bit and went out to find her friends near the river Murma. She found Tahu engrossed in profound thought, people who made great sacrifices for all this to happen. Nalia went up to her and sat down beside.

"Tahu, how did you do it?" Nalia asked.

"He slept. Slept like a baby, napping in the afternoon in the lap of the golden sun streaming though his latticed window. I was there walking past. I saw an axe placed against a coconut tree near his house. Took it. Went inside. Nobody saw me. I went straight into his room. The door was not bolted. I heard him snoring first. Then, I proceeded cautiously towards his bed. It was a high, ornate, expensive bed. I pulled the blanket off carefully, then I began to scythe him on his waist first and then his head and neck until blood began to gush from his body. The bed, the sheets the pillows everything turned red until it dripped from the bed so much so that it didn't matter anymore. He was practically cut in half when he screamed out in pain. Before people rushed in, I finished the job and walked out. No one saw me. After that, I heard that he had been taken to the hospital first for a bandage and then returned to the gravedigger for a decent burial. He still smelled of Dettol at the time of his burial. Babu, the apparition then scared his relatives out of the house by showing his nuance and making ghoulish echoes until they were convinced that this house was haunted and that they could not live here anymore.

"Oh, Tahu. Stop. Please stop. No more. No more of this."

Tahu cried, then she laughed unsteadily, pulled her dreadlocks by holding them in a bunch until it hurt. She looked over Murma, smiled and then stood up and started walking straight into the river. Nalia went after her.

"Stop! Tahu. Stop walking into the river. Please stop."

Tahu did not respond. She continued to walk through the watery passage. Wind picked up over the rippling water. Nalia tried to hold her back. But Tahu pushed her away. Nalia was not a match for her super-normal strength. She fell into the water with head down. And when she raised her head, only a few strands of Tahu's dreadlocks were visible in the notch of the waves. After that there was nothing besides the heaving waters. River that had seen mass exodus, deaths, and weddings, murmured quietly these eternal stories of the natives, also in the end engulfed Tahu. It seemed to have paved her way for atonement of the horrific crime. Pael came running to the river and a small group was gathered, as Nalia stood waling and sobbing in the deep water. Some said, her days of madness have finally ended,' others cried,' crazy woman will now finally rest in peace with her son.' But Nalia and Pael heard none of this. They kept searching and screaming for an answer, 'why did this happen? Why did it have to end like this? Where was God?

Who was going to rescue them? Oh the horror!' Cassandra's darkest calls during the Trojan War couldn't stop Agamemnon. Once set on its course, it couldn't be deterred regardless of her most profound prophesies. That was the inevitable nature of all tragedy. Ones that occurred in the Lost Winds were no different. They too were destined to happen and were just as uncontainable.

Tahu took revenge on her friend's behalf. She killed, but she also saved lives; lives that all the police and the harsh regime put together couldn't, which was why MD could return to the village today. Sooner or later there would be others, more and more. Characters who wanted to come back to homeland. No one knew how long before the next exodus would take place. The cold voice of reason perhaps wouldn't prevail, as didn't Cassandra's powerful words. Our societies were blind and deaf that paid little or no attention to wisdom and truth. Let alone act upon them. Epic battles retold such stories of folly only once too often. Maa was not there anymore to share the good news of Pontu's freedom into the Draviland community; not that she would be particularly overjoyed to know his current status. His case had to be exceptional. Unless Pontu was a brilliant tennis or a chess player or married a citizen purely out of love, he wouldn't be able to secure permanent permit. It almost seemed unlikely, given the rules for a rider. Protection on the basis of other grim realities was an option over which the high counsellor deliberated. This was if he feared death, persecution or horrible treatment on return by his enemies who might be a neighbour or a brother. Yet more rules existed such as persecution for reasons such as caste, creed, or free speech.

MD's news was better. He was coming back to the village to marry Pael.

People gathered one sunny winter morning by the river Murma one year after Tahu became an element of nature. A boat had just arrived and a man in his early 40's stepped out. Of course, it was MD. He wore a red and yellow bright full shirt and green full pants buttoned all the way up to the collar. Nalia rushed to greet him containing her excitement, while the others were not too forthcoming. There were smiles despite everything. The prodigal son had returned after all, who had given up his religion for nothing.

"How're you brother?" Nalia asked mildly.

"I'm well. What about you?"

"We're all well."

"I'm home."

MD looked around and was glad to see that the entire village had come here. But he wasn't too sure if they had come to greet him or simply out of curiosity. Nevertheless, they greeted him somewhat reluctantly and followed him to his house down the dirt path. MD looked around the green blades of rice in the fields leaning against the morning breeze. A flute played a distinctive familiar tune that he hadn't heard in many years. Smells of the earth and the winds ran a nostalgic note through his mind. They entered the same house that he had left so many years ago in anger. He saw Nalia's pink knitting resting tentatively on a chair in the front yard of the house. MD smiled and picked it up. Then he sat down. People spoke of nothing but gazed at him like a Martian put on a pedestal for display. He probably did look like one to them now that he had more personality. His character lines appeared deeply on his forehead; furrows in the cheeks and the chin along his fine chiselled bones. The blackness of his hair had been replaced with a shade of white grey down his side burns. He even wore a gold spectacle and a gold watch which clashed markedly with everything silvery-sh about him now; his dark complexion was set against the salt and pepper hair colour; same shade of moustache on his dark upper lips.

Nalia's mother became busy making innumerable cups of white sweet tea. The villagers sat down cross-legged on the ground facing MD without batting an eye-lid. Their curious eyes travelled all over his face and body. Nevertheless, he felt relieved at the prospect that no one had come running after him with an axe yet. His problem had been resolved as best as it could be. At the end of the day, he was a winner who had won every notable battle regardless. Victory was his and that was more than what one could say for others.

Hapless boat mates of MD's had been returned home for various reasons. Mostly because they had not met the eligibility criteria for riders; their stories just didn't add up. One case was of slightly different nature, however. Boys would sometimes fall in love with girls working for them in various capacities within the courts. They would try and win them with gifts, which those girls would refuse straightaway. Heart-broken, they volunteered to come back home, no matter how uncertain their futures were. Such were cases of love stories where unrelinquished passions ran high in every aspect sometimes driving boys to anger and madness, causing them to be thrown back into boot camp for violating the laws of the Draviland.

Lunch was underway; a feast would be served soon. Nalia's mother and her friends, Tahu's aunt and Nalia herself gathered together to do the cooking. Celebrations were underway. Lost Winds hadn't seen one like his since Nalia's wedding. MD excused himself to get out. The Fresh air in this place always surprised him, no matter what else had happened. He sauntered, through the village but felt the eyes of everyone on his back. Destination being the Banyan tree, he slowly made his way towards it. He saw someone just hide behind a massive oak.

"Who's there?" MD called out.

"Just me," replied the gravedigger as he came out of the hiding.

"I know who you're looking for. She waits for you too."

"You? How are you?"

"Good. How about you?"

"I'm well too. I have come a long way."

"I know."

"You do? How do you know?"

"I dreamt of you last night."

"What did you dream?"

"That you had just buried the past."

"Really? And what about you? Are you done digging graves yet?"

"For now yes. For a while. One job where business is always good."

"Yeah. You'll never be out of work. You'll outlive us all."

The gravedigger laughed oddly and told him that Pael waited for him under the Banyan tree. MD viewed the tree from a distance. It looked exactly the same as he had left it. It even had the noose still looped up around one of its short branches from the times that they had played as children. Swings went forward and backwards with every push. Somehow, he only went forward and never looked back again. He saw Pael's profile silhouetted as she looked at the sky unwittingly; her dark angelic beauty; sharp nose, thin lips and deer eyes. She hadn't aged a day, MD thought. The long black braid rested as usual on Pael's back like a black adder. MD crept up behind her and scissored her broad braid between the index and the middle fingers. Pael felt a tug, and turned around. They both faced each other quietly and remained looking for a long time; sipping out of the cup of joy, the tender moments of delightful love in infinite profusion.

"You couldn't write a single letter in all this time?"

"I did. It was lost in the wind."

"I heard that you called Nalia finally."

"Yes. I did.

"You haven't aged a day."

"More true in your case. You haven't aged a day either," he added enthusiastically.

"Tell me. Tell me about you. Tell me about us."

"It's all in my journal. Every single word in it came from my heart."

"My heart said you would come, even in the moment of greatest peril," Pael smiled.

"You waited."

"I waited."

"I love you Pael."

"You kept your promise."

"I did, because I could."

"Do you think I'd fit in the new country."

"No, not straightaway. But you'll learn. Everybody learns."

"I prayed for you."

"And He answered your prayers."

"What's the likelihood of that happening?"

"Don't know."

"Don't know."

"Pure luck?"

"Maybe, don't know. Let's talk about us."

He put his index finger over her lips and then kissed them. They stood under the tree in each other's embrace for such a long time that the trance wasn't quite broken until they heard Nalia giggle from behind. He smiled at her and so did Pael. Then they all sat under the tree on those bulky, knotty roots and started to talk; talks that he had been yearning to have with Nalia ever since he arrived to Lost Winds. MD shared his stories of the new land both with Pael and Nalia, who listened engrossed. In the West Mountains, Angella still lived alone. Her relationship with him bonded into a strong friendship, although she grew frail by now. Angella promised that she would write to him. He promised to respond.

He never thought that a day would come when he would be back in the village to claim what he believed to be his; his land; his family; his love; above all his life. Since that day, years went by and he saw green fields transforming into glowing sheafs of golden corns and rice with the turn of each season. Pael aged, so did he in the village. Now he was in the place of the wealthy farmer himself. Nalia, father and mother all became a part of this rustic life. Call him a *sage* if you like, but his incredible journey of success resonated and inspired many in similar circumstances. For this onerous life, which was no more than *a quintessence of dust* in the end, people were willing make impossible sacrifices and take unimaginable risks, outcomes of which were often decreed by fate. However aspirations, dreams were some of the most powerful components that also held life from falling apart. They propelled it towards the fulfilment of a destiny. All those hard tests required to pass in the boot camp and outside in the Dravi community on this journey to the safe haven were worthy trade-offs thereof. The presence of the paradoxical absence of the **ONE,** and His selective random process as to who won and who didn't was one of those many unresolved puzzles. However, His existence was as immutable as the law of gravity to the faithful.

THE END

Praises:

Professor Paul B McNulty University College Dublin

Ever since James Joyce introduced the concept of "stream of consciousness," I have been fascinated by this literary technique. It was against this background that I eagerly approached "Moirae" written by Mehreen Ahmed. I was not disappointed as she traversed the silent land of the Lost Winds. I loved the description of the arrest of Nalia's newly wedded husband as the police discovered the huge sum of money he had stolen. I was fascinated to find banshees in India which I had thought were unique to Ireland and Highland Scotland. I was also intrigued to find that her disgraced husband was found profiteering from illegal transportation of people fleeing from persecution, shades of our current problems in the Mediterranean. Ms Ahmed now had my undivided attention as I sailed through a most enjoyable read.

Tony McMahon, School of Media and Communication, RMIT University

Mehreen Ahmed is a wildly interesting writer. Moirae is not the first book from the Queensland scribe that I've read, but it is undoubtedly the best, most mature work. This is a nebulous yet - paradoxically perhaps – razor sharp text that speaks to the reader on a number of intellectual levels. Ahmed somehow manages to blend stream of consciousness type prose with a sure knack for story telling, and the results are no less than delightful. If you think about it, this kind of mixture is one that few writers have the ability – or the audacity – to attempt. Joyce is one exception that springs to mind, but he is probably an exception that only proves the rule. Jack Kerouac maybe. Either way, with this work, it is obvious that Ahmed joins a very select group indeed. Thoroughly recommended for both its technical beauty and, not inconsiderably, its bravery.

CPSIA information can be obtained
at www.ICGtesting.com
Printed in the USA
LVHW111659111119
637002LV00003B/456/P

9 781539 074878